'Um...doesn't your wife cook?' she asked, but the idea didn't last.

She almost forgot the question before it was out of her mouth. The heat of the fire, the morphine and the events of the night were catching up with her. Her words were slurring.

He smiled back at her. 'You want to concentrate on staying awake 'til your bed's made?'

She tried. But as he lifted her over onto the fresh sheets, as he drew the blankets over her, she felt her lids drooping and no amount of effort could keep them from closing.

'Thank you,' she murmured. It seemed enormously important to say it. 'Thank you for everything.'

'My pleasure,' he said, in an odd, thoughtful voice. 'It's all my pleasure, Dr Carmody. You go to sleep and don't worry about a thing.'

He touched her face. There it was again—this... strangeness. It was a tiny gesture, and why it should seem so personal...so right...

There was no figuring it out. She was too tired to try.

'G'nigh…' she whispered.

Marion Lennox is a country girl, born on an Australian dairy farm. She moved on—mostly because the cows just weren't interested in her stories! Married to a 'very special doctor', Marion writes Medical Romances™ as well as Mills & Boon® Romance. (She used a different name for each category for a while—if you're looking for her past Mills & Boon® Romance, search for author Trisha David as well.) She's now had 75 romance novels accepted for publication.

In her non-writing life Marion cares for kids, cats, dogs, chooks and goldfish. She travels, and she fights her rampant garden (she's losing) and her house dust (she's lost). Having spun in circles for the first part of her life, she's now stepped back from her 'other' career, which was teaching statistics at her local university. Finally she's reprioritised her life, figured out what's important, and discovered the joys of deep baths, romance and chocolate. Preferably all at the same time!

Recent titles by the same author:

A BRIDE AND CHILD WORTH WAITING FOR**
WANTED: ROYAL WIFE AND MOTHER†
HIS ISLAND BRIDE*
A ROYAL MARRIAGE OF CONVENIENCE†

*Mills & Boon® Medical™ Romance
**Crocodile Creek
†Mills & Boon® Romance

A SPECIAL KIND OF FAMILY

BY

MARION LENNOX

™ MILLS & BOON®

Pure reading pleasure™

First published in Great Britain 2009
Harlequin Mills & Boon Limited,
Eton House, 18-24 Paradise Road, Richmond, Surrey TW9 1SR

© Marion Lennox 2009

ISBN: 978 0 263 20799 6

Set in Times Roman 10 on 11½ pt
07-0609-53122

Printed and bound in Great Britain
by CPI Antony Rowe, Chippenham, Wiltshire

A SPECIAL KIND OF FAMILY

To my Number One Marion, my Number One Reader,
my Number One Mum.
Love you for ever.

CHAPTER ONE

THE doorbell rang at one in the morning. Dominic Spencer, Doc to the locals, swore and thumped his basin of dough into the trash. The locals knew he couldn't go out tonight. Was a patient coming to him?

Happy Easter, he thought, and tried not to glower as he stomped through the hall to the front door. It had better be serious.

It was.

The girl standing on his veranda was a bedraggled, muddy mess. Age? Somewhere between twenty and thirty. It was hard to be more precise. She was five feet six or so, slightly built, and wearing jeans and a windcheater, both coated with mud, and with blood. One leg of her jeans was ripped to the knee, and there was blood on her bare shin.

What else? She was wearing one filthy shoe, but only one. The other foot was partly covered by a sock, but the sock had long abandoned the idea of being footwear.

Her brown-black curls were drooping in sodden tendrils to her shoulders. Her eyes were huge. Scared. A long scratch ran from her left eyebrow almost to her chin, bleeding sluggishly.

She was carrying one of the ugliest dogs he'd ever seen. Maybe an English bulldog? Fat to the point of grotesque, it lay limply in her arms—a dead weight.

'Oh, thank God,' the girl managed before he had a chance to

speak. She shoved the dog forward, lurching like she was drunk. He grabbed the dog, then watched in dismay as she sank onto the veranda, put her head between her knees and held her head down with both hands.

Triage, he thought, his arms full of dog. Woman first, dog second. Get rid of the dog.

Rain was blasting in from the east, reaching almost to the door, so he turned and laid the dog on the mat inside the hall. The dog sagged like a rag doll, but the girl was his priority.

'What's wrong?' He caught her wrist. Her pulse was racing. She was sweating, and as he knelt beside her she started to retch.

'H-help me,' she stuttered, and couldn't manage more.

A child's sand bucket was lying on the veranda. He hauled it forward but she didn't need it. This hadn't been the first time she'd vomited tonight, then.

Now wasn't the time for questions. He did a more careful visual examination as he waited for the nasty little interlude to be over.

She was kneeling, which meant the damage to her leg must be superficial. The scratch on her face wasn't deep either. She was moving her arms freely. There didn't seem to be any major injury.

Maybe she was retching from exhaustion. If he'd had to carry that lump of a dog far, he might be retching, too.

This afternoon had been sultry before the change, and the kids had set up their paddling pool by the sandpit. A house-proud man might have tidied the place as soon as the colder weather hit, but housework was well down Dominic's list of priorities. So towels still lay on the veranda, albeit damp ones. As she ceased retching, he used one to wipe the worst of the mud and blood from her face. She submitted without reaction and he thought again, This is exhaustion.

'Let's get you inside.'

She looked up then, as if seeing him for the first time. 'Where…where…?' She was almost incoherent.

'I'm the local doctor,' he said, smiling at her in what he

hoped was his best bedside manner. 'I assume you know that from the sign on the front gate. My name's Dominic Spencer. Dom for short.'

'Dominic,' she managed.

'Dom will do fine. And your name?

'Erin Carmody.'

It wasn't a comprehensive patient history but it'd do for now. 'What hurts?'

'Everything.' It was practically a wail and he relaxed a little. In his experience, patients who were deathly ill didn't wail.

'Anything specific?'

'N-no.'

'What happened?'

'I crashed my car.'

Where? The roads round here would be deserted at this time of night. Where had she walked from?

'Is anyone else hurt?' he asked, and she managed to shake her head.

'So there's no one else at the car.'

'N-no. I was by myself.'

'Is the car obstructing the road? Do I need to call the police?'

'No.'

'Okay. Let's get you out of the rain where I can take a look at you.'

'I shouldn't be here,' she managed. 'It's really late.' She stared blindly up at him and he thought he saw fear. Her eyes were wide and brown and shocked.

It was one in the morning. Maybe reassurance was the way to go.

'Take a look around,' he said gently, motioning to the jumble behind him—buckets and spades, Nathan's tricycle, Martin's pogo stick, the bundle of wet towels left from the day's play. 'I'm a dad as well as a doctor. My kids are asleep upstairs. You're safe here.'

'The dog…'

'Even the dog's safe with me,' he said ruefully. 'Safe, reliable Dr Spencer.'

She even managed a smile at that. 'Don't say it like you'd rather be a playboy,' she whispered.

'Leave my fantasies alone,' he growled, and smiled back. 'Now, Erin, don't get your knickers in a knot but I'm going to carry you indoors. One, two, three, go.' And before she could protest he swung her up into his arms.

She was older than twenty. She was every bit a woman, he thought as his arms held her close. Pushing thirty? Maybe. Now the worst of the mess was gone from her face he could see smile lines around her eyes. Or worry lines? Nope, smile lines, he thought. She had clear, brown eyes, nicely spaced. Her mouth was generous and her nose was decidedly cute.

That was hardly patient appraisal. He gave himself a swift mental swipe and carried her inside before she could find the strength to protest.

She did protest as he stepped over the dog in the hall.

'The dog…' she managed. 'Put me down.'

'I'll attend to your dog as soon as I've attended to you.' In fact, he wouldn't be surprised if the dog was on the way out. It hadn't moved an inch since he'd set it down.

But that wasn't his concern right now. Erin had been retching. He needed to check there wasn't a ruptured spleen or something equally appalling going on inside. So he stepped over the limp dog with purpose and carried her into the living room.

He'd been reading in here while he waited for his dough to…not rise. The open fire was still sending out warmth, making the place seem intimate and welcoming. The settee was big and squishy, built for comfort rather than style.

She protested again as he laid her on the mound of cushions.

'I can't. Your wife… I'll stain your settee,' she whispered as he laid her down, but her protest was weak. She was almost past arguing.

'I have kids,' he growled. 'We've given up worrying about Home Beautiful years ago. Let's have a look at you.'

There was a better light in the living room and he could see her more clearly. Lots of superficial injuries, he thought, taking in scratches and bruising. There was blood but not so much in any one place that it merited concern.

'Can we take the worst of those clothes off?' he asked, half expecting her to protest again, but she simply looked at him for a long moment, maybe assessing for herself the truth of his state-ment about reliability, steadfastness—dad material rather than playboy stuff. What she saw must have been okay. She nodded mutely and submitted as he peeled off her windcheater and tugged her jeans away.

He wanted her dry. Her bra and panties were scant and lacy—they'd dry quickly on her, he thought, and he guessed she'd be much happier if he let them be. He pulled a mohair throw from the back of the settee, tucked it round her and felt her relax a little with the warmth.

He felt her pulse again and it was slowing, growing stronger and steadier.

'How far did you carry the dog?' he asked, checking an arm gently, watching her face for reaction. No problems there. Her hands were scratched but there were no breaks. He lifted the other arm before she found the strength to reply.

'Miles,' she said, and she even managed to sound indignant. 'This is the middle of nowhere.'

'What, Bombadeen?' he asked, pseudo indignant to match. 'Bombadeen's the cultural capital of the known world.'

'Right,' she managed, and tried for a smile. Then, as he moved to check her legs she added, 'My legs are fine. Do you think I could have carried him with a broken leg?'

'Toes?'

'Also fine.'

But they weren't. He tugged the lone trainer off her right

foot. That was okay. He gently peeled the remainder of the sock from her left foot. Less than okay. Gravel was deeply embedded. The foot was bleeding, rubbed raw.

Not life-threatening, though. Move on for now.

'Tummy?'

'That does hurt,' she whispered, finally acknowledging pain. 'Like I've-just-been-retching hurt. But, no, I wasn't hit in the chest or abdomen. I'd imagine my kidneys and spleen are in one piece and I'm breathing okay.'

She had medical knowledge, then? He smiled but he didn't take her word for it. He put his hands gently on her abdomen and felt, still watching her face.

'It's true. I'm fine,' she whispered.

'In fact, you've never looked better,' he agreed, relaxing. Then triage kicked in again. 'You've been in a car accident. You're sure no one else was hurt?'

'There's only me.'

'And your car… You're sure it's not blocking the road? Do I need to call the emergency services to clear it?'

'It's way off the road,' she said, suddenly bitter. 'But even if it was, would you need to clear it? Apart from the car that caused me to crash—which didn't even stop—I've seen no other car for hours.'

'It's a quiet little town in the middle of coastal bushland—and we're on holiday.' He was still watching her face, thinking the situation through. What next?

In the warm room Erin's colour was starting to return. Her foot needed attention, as did her mass of cuts and bruises, but if she'd carried the dog for miles she must really care about it. Maybe triage said he ought to check.

'If you're okay for a minute, I'll see what's happening to your dog.'

'Would you?' She closed her eyes. 'I think he's dying. He was moving when I picked him up—he sort of moaned—but he didn't struggle.'

'I'll see what I can do,' Dom said, and put his hand on her cheek in a fleeting gesture of reassurance. 'Don't move.' He tucked the rug more tightly round her, pulled a couple more logs onto the fire then left, leaving the door wide so she could watch him.

Her eyes followed him. She must love the dog a lot to carry him with her foot like that, he thought. It'd be good if he could do something. But, like she'd said, the dog looked close to death.

The creature hadn't moved. Dom flicked the hall light on so he could see him better and stooped over the limp form.

He wasn't dead yet. Neither was he unconscious. The dog's eyes were huge. He looked up at Dominic and his expression was almost imploring.

If there was one thing Dom was a sucker for it was a dog, especially a dog in trouble. And this one was really in trouble. 'Hey,' Dominic said softly, and put a finger gently behind the dog's soft ear. He scratched gently. 'Hey, it's okay.'

He liked this dog on sight. It was mix of English bulldog and something he didn't know. Part bulldog, part mutt? Dog ugly in every sense of the word. He looked a bit like Winston Churchill, missing the cigar.

But he didn't smile at the thought. The situation was too serious.

Tending an injured dog had problems not normally associated with people, the main one being their propensity to bite. This one looked beyond biting, but Dom sensed that even when he was well this dog would be docile. His eyes followed him with absolute trust.

But, hell, he must be hurt. Why wasn't he moving?

A few months ago Dom had attended a guy who'd come off his bike onto gravel. That's what this dog looked like—he'd been dragged along the road. His coat was a mass of scratches, some deep. His mistress was in a much better state than he was.

What was so wrong that the dog couldn't move?

He'd laid the dog on the doormat and the dog had slumped so his legs were facing the wall. Now Dom carefully pulled the mat around—with dog attached—so he could get a clear view of the dog's joints. A smashed leg would explain immobility.

But his legs were fine. Or…not. Here at last was information to enter in his patient's history. In Dom's expert medical opinion, these were *her* legs.

'What's your dog's name?' he called back into the sitting room.

'You tell me and we'll both know,' the woman muttered, and Dominic thought he needed to give her something for pain.

But suddenly his attention switched back to the dog. For, as he watched, a ripple ran across its limp body. The muscle contraction was unmistakable.

From a little bit of information suddenly he had a lot of information. Too much. This dog was not male and she was not fat. *She* was heavily pregnant and by the look of her body she was in labour.

Great, Dom thought. Fantastic. Half an hour ago he'd been bored to snores. Now he had a wounded woman lying on his sitting-room settee, and a pregnant bitch who was showing every sign of dying unless he could do something about it. And the last vet had left Bombadeen back in 1980. Via the graveyard.

Okay, he needed a history. He rose, striding swiftly back into the sitting room. 'I need to know…' he started, but at the look on Erin's face he changed priorities again and headed for his surgery. That foot would be excruciatingly painful. His surgery was at the back of the house, accessed through his study. Two minutes later he was back, hauling his bag open, retrieving what he needed.

'Sorry,' he said, kneeling beside Erin and lifting the rug back a little. 'I shouldn't have let the dog distract me. I'm giving you something for the pain. Are you allergic to anything?'

'No, I—'

'No reaction to morphine?'

'No, but—'

'Then let's stop things hurting,' he said. He should set up a mask but he was forming priorities as he went. A mask meant he'd need to stay with her while she slowly gained the level of pain relief she needed. But he had a birth on his hands. She had brought the dog, after all.

'I don't need morphine,' she muttered.

'Tell me it's not hurting.'

She hesitated. Then, 'It's hurting,' she conceded.

'You came to the doctor's. I assume that's because you were looking for medical help.'

'Your house is the first house out of bushland. But when I saw your sign… I was looking for help with the dog.'

'I'm not a vet. I'll do my best for her, but—'

'Her?'

'Her. But we'll get you sorted first. I'll give you something to stop the vomiting as well.' He hesitated, his eyebrows still raised. Waiting for her agreement. She looked at the syringe. Then she winced again and nodded.

'I suspect you've been brave enough for a lifetime tonight,' he said gently, swabbing her thigh. 'I need to go back to your dog but can you quickly tell me what happened?'

'I'm on my way to Campbelltown,' she said, closing her eyes as the needle went in. Then opening them again. 'Hey, not bad. That hardly hurt.'

'I'm a doctor,' he said, and smiled. 'It's what I do. So then?'

She was still having trouble talking. Shock, exhaustion and fear had taken quite a toll. 'Anyway, I'd sort of deviated from the main Campbelltown route. I…I needed thinking time. So I didn't know the road. And then there was a car in front of me. An ancient car that trailed smoke. It was weaving as if the driver was drunk. It was just after dark. The road was narrow near the cliffs beside the river, and suddenly the rear door of the car opened and the dog was thrown out.'

'Thrown…'

'They pushed him,' she said, horror flooding into her voice as she recalled. 'Right into the path of my car. I would have hit him but I swerved.'

'You went over the cliff!' She must have. The road by the river left no room for error.

'What do you think?' she said bitterly. 'So my car was on its side right down the bottom of the cliff. I'm lucky I didn't go into the river. I lay in the car for a bit thinking someone would rescue me—I'm sure the people in the car in front must have seen what happened. But nothing. So finally I kicked my way out of the passenger door, which was suddenly my roof. It was really dark. My shoe came off and I couldn't find it. I couldn't find my phone. I climbed up the cliff but it took me ages and the dog was lying in the middle of the road. Just lying there. So I sat there in the dark, waiting to get my breath back—waiting for someone to come along. And I thought the dog was dying but he didn't die. So finally I picked him up and carried him here.'

'If you went over where I think you went over… That's two— maybe three miles you've walked,' Dominic said, horrified.

'It felt like ten.' She closed her eyes again. And then she opened them again. 'What?'

'Nothing. No, actually, not nothing. I'm thinking you deserve a medal. I can't believe…' He shook his head, forcing himself to move on. 'I need to go back to the dog.'

'The *she* dog,' she said cautiously. 'Elementary mistake. I guess my examination skills leave a bit to be desired.'

Definitely medical, he thought. Nurse? But now was hardly the time to ask.

'The she dog,' he agreed gravely. 'And I think I know why she's not moving.'

'Why?'

'She's in labour. I'm guessing by the look of her that she's been in labour for a while. I need to haul out my veterinary books and see what I can do. We'll give your injection time to work and I'll take a closer look at those scratches. Meanwhile…'

'Do your best,' she said, and managed a smile. 'I didn't pick she was a she and I didn't pick she was in labour. I deserve to be struck off. But please…help her. I haven't lugged her all this way to have her die.'

CHAPTER TWO

SHE might well have. The dog was still exactly as Dom had left her. He squatted beside her and winced.

She was an obvious stray. She wore a frayed collar with no identification. She'd been dumped. She looked emaciated and exhausted and ill almost to the point of death.

Maybe it would be more humane to put her down, he thought ruefully. As the only person with any medical knowledge for fifty miles, Dom had been called on for veterinarian duty in the past. He had something in his bag that would be fast and painless.

But…

But the dog was looking up at him. He'd never seen such pleading eyes.

He swallowed. It'd be sensible…

The dog's gaze wasn't leaving his face.

He watched as another contraction rippled through her body. It was weaker than the last. It was a wonder her contractions hadn't ceased altogether, given what she was going through.

He did a fast, basic examination. There was no sign of a puppy coming.

How long had the contractions been happening? Erin had obviously not been in a state to notice, but the fact that the second contraction was weaker than the first told its own story.

This was an abnormal labour, in a dog near death.

He couldn't do a Caesarean section. He'd learned a few basic vet skills, but this was way beyond him. He had no anaesthetist to help him. Even if could find out the dosage, what sort of anaesthetic could he give a bitch so close to death?

Erin's heroics aside, what was the sensible course of action?

She was a badly injured, stray dog in obstructed labour. He knew the logical thing to do.

But still her eyes pleaded.

Okay. Soft-touch Doc Dom. He sighed and hit his phone. Fiona McLay was the nearest vet, fifty miles away. She was as soft a touch as he was. Like Dom, Fiona was on call twenty-four hours a day, seven days a week. She was nearing seventy, she was wonderful, and when he was having a bad day he reminded himself that if Fiona could do it, so could he.

She answered on the first ring.

'Sorry to wake you, Fi,' he said. 'But I have a problem. Can you give me some advice?'

The morphine was starting to take effect. Finally. The pain in her foot and in her shoulders was taking a back step.

She was warm. Gloriously, safely warm. Dominic had loaded the fire, the flames were leaping and the room was fabulously heated. She was still a bit damp but it didn't matter.

She could go to sleep, right now.

She should ring Charles and her parents, she thought drowsily. They'd worry.

Or not. They'd just assume she'd been caught up at work. They certainly wouldn't be pacing.

They'd be furious with her anyway. Maybe they'd even expect her not to come.

'I'd kill her.'

Out in the hall Dom's voice sounded startled. Up until now she'd been concentrating on the pain, but now Erin lay back and let Dom's words sink in.

'If you're sure… Then I'm guessing it's been stuck for hours. Yeah, you're right, there's no choice. No, you're right there, too, she's not going to make it that far. Or that long. She'd be dead before you got here. Thanks for offering anyway, Fi, you're a hero. Okay, step by step. Yeah, I've got the kit you made up for me—not that I ever dreamed of using it. Talk me through it slowly. I'll write down dosages as we go.'

Silence followed. She peered around the back of the settee and saw him taking notes. Finally the receiver was replaced. She heard him moving away somewhere further down the hall, the sound of running water in the bathroom, then things being set up on the floorboards by the front door. Just out of sight.

'I know, girl,' he said, so softly she had to strain to hear. 'It's not a great operating table, but I don't want to move you more than I need to. And I've set up the desk lamp so I can see.'

This was killing her. She wiggled her foot with care. The worst of the throbbing had stopped. That was because she wasn't standing on it, she thought.

Okay, she wouldn't stand on it. She wrapped the rug around her, slid off the settee and wriggled on her backside over the floor. Her shoulders complained but what the heck—what was morphine for? She'd put too much into saving this dog to stop now.

She reached the doorway and peered round. Dom was intent on the dog. He'd set up a high bendy light so he could see. He was setting up a dripstand.

She paused, taking in the whole scene. Her dog was lying in the hallway. With the morphine aboard Erin could focus on her surroundings now, taking in the wide, old-fashioned hall, the high ceilings, the massive architraves. And she could also get a good look at this doctor. Dominic Spencer?

He was youngish, she thought. Mid-thirties? His dark chocolate-brown hair was a bit too long, a bit wavy, with some of it flopping down over one eye. Not too far—like he was a week or so overdue for a haircut. And a day or two late for a shave. And a year or so overdue for an iron. He looked rumpled, she thought. She was used to the men in her life being...groomed. This guy was wearing faded jeans, ancient trainers and an old cotton shirt with rolled-up sleeves and a frayed collar. His top two buttons had disappeared long since.

He didn't look like a doctor, she thought. If the sign on the brass plate out the front—plus his actions since she'd arrived—didn't bear out his introduction she'd have guessed maybe he was the doctor's artist-brother, who'd maybe cadged a bed over Easter because he was living on the smell of an oily rag.

But in what he was doing, this guy was proving every inch a doctor. His lean face looked absolutely focused.

He looked...wonderful. It must be the morphine talking, she thought, dazed. She didn't respond to men like this. Of all the stupid, hormonal reactions...

At least he hadn't noticed. With the drip started, Dom had turned his attention to his equipment.

'What are you doing?' she asked.

He glanced around—one swift glance that said he was completely preoccupied—then turned back to what he was doing. 'If you move you'll hurt yourself,' he said briefly. 'Go back to the settee.'

'I'm hurting because of this dog,' she said. 'I think I'll call her Marilyn.'

'Marilyn?'

'As in Monroe. 'Cos she's gorgeous and misunderstood.'

His mouth quirked into a trace of a smile. A damned attractive smile, her hormones said.

No, she told her hormones.

'Marilyn it is, then,' he agreed. Then his smile died. 'But I need to tell you she's not likely to make it.'

'I can't believe I didn't pick up that she was in labour. I thought she was just fat.'

'You're hurt yourself.' He turned back to her, refocusing. 'Go back to the settee,' he said. 'Please. This won't be pretty.'

'You're not putting her down?'

'Not yet.' He motioned to the drip. 'I'm getting some fluid on board. She's still having weak contractions. My guess—and I've just spoken to the vet in the next town and she concurs—is that she's been in labour for some time. We think she's got a pup stuck. Maybe that's why she was dumped. Maybe she got into trouble giving birth, someone said they'd take her to the vet—maybe to keep kids happy—and then they dumped her. Taking a pregnant bitch to the vet costs money.' His face tightened. 'Dumping her would be easier. Throwing her out where you said they did—my guess is they intended her to go in the river. It's only a guess, but people can be cruel.'

He spoke like he knew what he was talking about. He spoke like a man with ghosts. She registered it, but only fleetingly. Her foot was hurting, her hormones had taken a back seat to discomfort, and she only had so much registering space possible.

'So what are you doing?'

'Trying to get the pup out.'

'A Caesarean?'

'I can't. She's so weak it'd kill her even if I had the skills—which I don't.'

'Neither do I,' she said regretfully. 'I'm an accident and emergency consultant.'

'You're a doctor?' he demanded, clearly astounded.

'I am.' She wriggled closer. He was loading a syringe. 'What is that?'

'Lubricant,' he said, and the surprise he'd shown disappeared as he turned back to what he was doing. He was carefully filling a syringe full of gel. Then he moved, deliberately blocking her view.

'You'll kill the puppy,' she said, appalled. How could he manoeuvre lubricant into a blocked birth canal without…?

'The pup will be dead anyway,' he said flatly. He was speaking almost to himself. 'Fiona...my vet friend...tells me if it's been wedged for hours there's no chance it's still alive. She tells me I have a choice. I put Marilyn down now, or I try and get the dead pup out of the birth canal so whatever's behind can come out of its own accord. If it doesn't work then I'll have to put her down, but I intend to try. So if you could shut up...'

'I'm shutting up,' she said, and pushed herself forward a bit more. 'But you have an assistant. I may not be sterile but I'll do whatever I can to help.'

It was a nasty procedure with an initial nasty outcome. Dom inserted the lubricant with difficulty. He injected oxytocin. He used forceps with even more difficulty. He fitted the forceps just as a contraction hit. He tugged. The thing shifted and suddenly it was there. Just as Fiona had foreseen.

He glanced back at Erin, who was lying full length on the floor, keeping a light touch on Marilyn's carotid artery, feeling her pulse, and stroking her ears. 'One pup,' he told her softly. 'Dead.'

Amazingly, Marilyn struggled, raising her head as if to see. She moaned, a low doggy moan that sounded almost like despair.

'Hush,' Erin said softly, fondling the big dog's ears as Dom removed the dead puppy. 'I know, it's your baby and I'm so sorry, but you did the best you could. Relax, girl. We'll take care of it.'

Her bedside manner was great, Dom thought, though it was slightly more personal than the approach he'd learned in medical school. She was lying nose to nose with her patient.

'And you moaned,' Erin whispered. 'That's the first sound you've made since I found you. That has to be good.' She glanced up at Dom again. 'What's happening?

'I'd imagine this pup died in utero some time ago,' Dom said grimly, wrapping the tiny body in a towel and placing it gently to one side. 'It's not completely formed and it's stiff. That's why it's blocked the birth passage.'

'If they're all like that…'

'The oxytocin's only so good at getting the contractions going again,' he muttered. 'We need a bit of luck…'

He stopped.

The pressure behind the dead pup must have been overwhelming. The contraction Marilyn was having now was almost nonexistent, but it was enough. A wobbly, limp body was propelled outward in a rush. Dom caught it as it came—and the tiny bundle moved in his hand.

Again, Marilyn tried to turn. 'It's okay, girl,' Erin whispered. 'Leave your babies to Dr Dom. He's doing it all for you. We're both in his hands.'

What was in Dom's hands was a live pup. Dom peeled membrane away from one tiny nose. He held the tiny creature upside down and gave it a faint jiggle.

It gave a sound that could almost have been…a bark?

'Dear God,' Erin said, and burst into tears.

'You cry, you're out of my theatre, Dr Carmody,' Dom said, but he was grinning. 'Some surgical assistant you are.' He headed down the hall with the pup in his hands. 'Don't let her have another contraction till I come back.'

He needed warm towels. Hell, he'd never anticipated a live birth. Luckily he had heated towel rails in the bathroom. He grabbed the family towels, wrapped the pup in one and tucked another two towels under his arm.

By the time he got back to the hall Erin had his doctor's bag tipped out on the floor. 'Dental floss,' she murmured in approval as she searched. 'You're a man after my own heart. What sort of doctor doesn't carry dental floss?'

He grinned, then laid the pup on a towel on the floor right near Marilyn's head.

'Do we need to clamp and tie the umbilical cord?' Erin asked doubtfully.

'You're asking me as a dog expert? Let's do it anyway.' Then, as another contraction rippled through, he left the pup to Erin and went back to delivery mode.

And two pups later it was over. At least he guessed it was over. There was no heartbeat that he could hear inside—there were no signs that there were any more to come. The third live pup slid into the world and Marilyn's body seemed to sag in relief.

'Don't you dare die now,' Erin said to her, almost fiercely. 'Dr Dom's getting fluids into you. He's doing everything he can. You have three puppies totally dependent on you. You can't die.'

Not completely dependent, Dom thought ruefully as he watched Erin. Marilyn was lying back, exhausted to the point of death, but as Erin presented each of her pups to her she nosed them with the beginning of maternal interest. As Erin set them at their mother's teats, they knew what to do.

Erin was doing everything she could to give these puppies a start in life, and Marilyn was trying herself. The big dog was breathing deeply, evenly, as if she guessed that she had to concentrate on gathering her strength.

'She's a dog in a million,' Erin said fiercely, echoing his thoughts. 'How can they have just thrown her out?'

'It beggars belief,' Dom said sadly. 'But that's life. We just pick up the pieces.'

'You sound like you do it all the time.'

'I'm a family doctor.'

'Yeah, family.' She gazed up at him, seeming suddenly to realise that she was semi-naked, lying full length in the hall of…a family doctor. A doctor with a family. 'Um…how come we haven't woken your wife and kids?'

Maybe now wasn't the time to let her know exactly what his family consisted of, Dom thought. He needed her settled tonight, and if the thought of a wife and kids upstairs would do it, then that's what she'd get. 'I'm a family doctor,' he repeated, with tired humour. 'In this family we learn to sleep with bombs going off—or sometimes that's what it feels like. I nap between explosions. Now…' He looked down at Marilyn, who was almost visibly relaxing. Her eyes were three-quarters closed. The puppies were a living, breathing pile of life, nuzzling her teats. The fire in the living room was sending its warmth out here. Marilyn was safe, and she was delivered.

'You know what? I'm going to leave her right here,' Dom said. 'I'll put a heater out here to make it even warmer, but she looks like she'll sleep for hours and I don't want that IV line to move. In the morning I'll do something about cleaning up her side but it looks like superficial scratches. Fiona told me what antibiotic to give. I'll clean the mess up later.' He rose. 'Which means…' He looked down at Erin, who was smiling goofily at the pups. 'You,' he said. 'Feet. I'm not leaving them till morning.'

'I'm fine.'

'That's right,' he agreed. 'You're nicely doped on morphine and you could walk another three miles or so. Or not. Dr Carmody, you know very well that your foot has to be attended to, and it has to be attended to now.'

There was nothing to say. Even if there was a decent rebuttal she was too tired and too drugged to think of one.

'Yes, Doctor,' she said meekly, and held out her hands so he could help her to her feet.

He didn't.

'You've walked far enough tonight,' he growled. ''You need to come through to my surgery at the back of the house.' And before she could guess what he intended—or protest—he picked her up again and was carrying her through the house to his clinic beyond.

What followed was nasty. Dom gave her as much analgesic as he could, but short of a general anaesthetic—'and I'm not doing that on my own'—he couldn't stop all the pain.

There was gravel, deeply embedded. She'd felt pain as she'd walked but there hadn't been a choice. She'd just kept on walking.

'Any other night there'd be traffic on that road,' he told her.

'But it's the Thursday before Easter. The whole town's either left for holidays or hunkered down with visitors.'

He was trying to distract her. She lay back and tried really hard not to think about what he was doing. He was making sure not one trace of gravel remained.

'So why aren't you either on holidays or hunkered down with visitors?'

'Hey, I am,' he said, smiling suddenly. She liked it a lot when he smiled, she decided. Normally his face looked strained. Like life was hard. But when he smiled the sun came out. It made her feel…silly. No, she chided herself. That was the morphine. One man's smile shouldn't make her feel silly. She was a very serious person. Or she would be if he'd stop smiling.

'One woman with a sore foot,' he was saying. 'One dog and three puppies. That makes visitors. Pity about the Easter buns.'

'The Easter buns?'

'They didn't rise,' he said sorrowfully. 'I'm in all sorts of trouble. But don't you worry about me. You just think about your own worries. Crashed car. Injured foot. Bruises all over and a messed-up holiday to boot. You keep thinking about them and let me get on with my own troubles. Easter buns as flat as pancakes.'

She chuckled. The sound surprised them both. He glanced up at her and grinned and then he went back to what he was doing. Ouch. Her smile faded. She bit her lip, then decided she needed to smile again. Suddenly it seemed really important to keep smiling.

'It's okay not to be a martyr,' he said gently. 'Swear if you want.'

'I don't swear,' she said with an attempt at dignity.

'I chop things.'

'Pardon?'

'I have an axe,' he said. 'When life gets tough—when things go wrong or when Gloria Fisher comes in with her something's-wrong-with-me-middle complaint for the fourth time in a week and she still refuses to stop wearing too-tight corsets—I go outside and chop anything that comes to hand. Luckily there's lots of old tree stumps on this place. I keep the family in firewood year round.'

'Venting spleen?'

'That's the one,' he said cheerfully. 'If you like I'll let you borrow my axe. Only not tonight.'

And then, magically, he set aside his instruments. 'All done. Now there's nothing else you're not telling me about? Pain-wise?'

'I… No.'

'You swear?'

'My shoulders ache from carrying Marilyn. I suspect I'll ache for a bit but I was well strapped in when the car rolled. I really will be okay.'

'So who do we phone to come and get you?'

She blinked. She hadn't thought that far ahead.

Charles. Her parents. Charles's parents. Of course she should ring them. But it was, what, three in the morning, and they were angry with her already.

'Family?' he asked, and she nodded. Her parents were with Charles and Charles's parents. The whole domestic catastrophe— except the one element that was supposed to complete the whole.

The pig in the middle. A small, rebellious pig.

'You know, if you were heading to your parents' for Easter and don't want to wake them—if you're sure they won't be worrying—you're welcome to sleep here,' he said gently, watching her face. 'I don't want to move your dog until morning anyway. The settee's as big as a bed and the fire's comforting.'

She thought of the alternative. Ringing Charles. Waking Charles's parents and her parents; scaring them with the news of another accident. They'd send Charles to fetch her. He'd be kind and supportive and not offer a word of reproach until she was over her shock. And… Taking Marilyn?

Aaagh.

Dom must be reading her face. He placed a last piece of dressing on her foot and touched her lightly on her ankle. It was a feather touch of reassurance, and why it had the capacity to make her feel reassured she had no idea. But, unaccountably, it did.

'Hey, no drama,' he said. 'Your settee's practically made for you anyway. But I do need a guarantee that no one will be looking for you.'

'Not…my family. They'll assume I stayed in Melbourne until the morning.' They might even assume she'd decided not to come at all, she thought ruefully. She darn near hadn't. 'But if those yahoos saw me go over the cliff…'

'They may have reported it. It's unlikely, or you'd have been found before this. I'll ring the local police and tell them if anyone reports a crashed car I have the driver safe. Okay. All sorted. And now the driver needs to sleep.'

And before she knew it, once again she was in his arms. Was this how country doctors transported patients? The thought made her feel silly again.

'What?' he asked as he carried her through the silent house.

The man was percipient, she thought. She'd allowed herself a tiny smile, meant only for herself, but he'd picked up on it.

'I'm just thinking most hospitals have trolleys.'

'Yeah, and hospital orderlies,' he said with wry humour. 'And nurses and regulations about lifting and role demarcation. But orderlies are in short supply around here. So lie back, pretend to be a really light suitcase and let me do my job.'

The man was seriously efficient. He set her in an armchair for a couple of minutes, disappeared and came back with linen, pillows and blankets. She watched as he made up her bed— faster than she'd thought possible. The man had real domestic skills. Except in making Easter buns.

'Um…doesn't your wife cook?' she asked, but the idea didn't last. She almost forgot the question before it was out of her mouth. The heat of the fire, the morphine and the events of the night were catching up with her. Her words were slurring.

He smiled back at her. 'You want to concentrate on staying awake till your bed's made.'

She tried. But as he lifted her over onto the fresh sheets, as he drew the blankets over her, she felt her lids drooping and no amount of effort could keep them from closing.

'Thank you,' she murmured. It seemed enormously important to say it. 'Thank you for everything.'

'My pleasure,' he said in an odd, thoughtful voice. 'It's all my pleasure, Dr Carmody. You go to sleep and don't worry about a thing.'

He touched her face. There it was again—this…strangeness. It was a tiny gesture and why it should seem so personal…so right…

There was no figuring it out. She was too tired to try.

'G'nigh'…' she whispered.

She slept.

He should start Easter buns again. It was not much after three in the morning after all.

Yeah, right. Sod the buns.

He crouched by Marilyn for a bit, watching her breathe in, breathe out.

'You keep on doing that,' he told her, and she opened her big eyes. She looked up at him, and amazingly her tail moved, just a fraction.

'You're wonderful,' he told her. 'Just like your mistress.'

Her tail moved again.

'Hey, that's enough effort,' he told her. 'Go to sleep.'

He watched as she did just that. She was a wreck, he thought, a disaster washed up on the jagged rocks of human cruelty. Like so many disasters. He had two of them sleeping upstairs right now.

Could he keep Marilyn as well? Could he keep three pups?

Not and keep working, he thought bleakly. But, hey, they all might find homes. Scrubbed and cared for, Marilyn might look quite…attractive?

Um…no. This dog couldn't look attractive in a million years. No matter what the care.

Would Erin take her?

But he'd watched Erin's face as he'd said she shouldn't move the dog tonight, the inference being when she moved so would the dog. He'd seen dismay.

'So it's up to me again,' he told Marilyn, but then he gave himself a mental swipe to the side of the head. 'Hey, that's me being despondent. There'll be all sorts of people just aching to give you a good home. A nice brick bungalow with room to romp, a couple of dog-loving kids, balls to chase, a pile of dog food so high you can't see the top…'

He glanced into the sitting room toward the sleeping Erin. Was she the girl to provide it?

Maybe not. But, then, he thought, still hopeful, he'd really liked what he'd seen. For now he'd indulge his very own personal philosophy. Which was to worry about tomorrow tomorrow.

Finding homes for puppies was for tomorrow. Flat Easter buns were for tomorrow. Tonight—or what was left of it—was for sleep.

And maybe for letting himself think just a little bit about what sort of woman carried an injured dog so far…

CHAPTER THREE

SHE woke and she was being watched. She opened one eye, looked sideways at the door and two small heads ducked for cover.

She closed her eyes and waited for a bit. Testing herself out. She wiggled everything, really cautiously. Various protests started up in response, but compared to the pain of last night they were minor.

Then she wiggled her left foot and thought, no, not minor.

She opened her eyes again. Once more, two heads, but this time they didn't withdraw.

One head was bright, carrot red, really curly. The other was mousy brown, dead straight.

Five or six years old, she guessed, and then she thought they didn't look one bit like the man who'd helped her last night.

'Hi,' she said, and the redhead gave a nervous smile. He was the oldest. The younger one ducked back behind the door.

'Dom said we're not to wake you,' Red-head said.

Dom. Hmm.

'Dom's your dad?'

'Sort of,' Red-head said, most unsatisfactorily. 'He's in the kitchen making breakfast. The buns didn't work.' This sounded like a tragedy of epic proportions.

'But we've got puppies,' the other little boy said from the anonymity of behind the door. 'Only Dom said we're not allowed to wake them, either.'

'Well, I'm awake,' Erin said, swinging her feet off the settee. Putting her right foot cautiously to the floor. Wondering if she dared do anything with her left foot. 'Did your dad tell you I hurt my feet last night?'

'He said you crashed your car off the cliff and you saved the dog by carrying her for miles and miles.' Red-head was looking at her like he might look at Superman.

'It was nothing,' she said modestly. And then… 'Um…if you guys got on either side of me I might be able to make it to the kitchen.'

'You want us to help?' Red-head said.

'I do.'

They thought about it. Finally Red-head nodded. 'Okay,' he said. 'Come on, Nathan. We gotta help. I'm Martin,' he added.

'I'm pleased to meet you, Martin,' she said. 'And Nathan. Can you help me hop?'

Nathan's head appeared again. 'Sometimes I help my mum go to the bathroom,' he said, sounding wise far beyond his years. 'Do you want us to help you to the bathroom?'

He was a child in a million.

'Yes, please,' she said gratefully, and a minute later she had a small, living crutch at each side. She was on her way, via the bathroom, to meet the doctor's family.

They'd be ready at lunchtime. Maybe.

What sort of father forgot to buy Easter buns? Well, okay, he hadn't forgotten, but he had forgotten to put in an order, he hadn't reached the shops until three and they'd been sold out. So he'd thought, no problem, he'd buy yeast and make 'em. Piece of cake.

Not quite. Not even on this, his second try. And he ought to check on Erin.

The door swung open. Erin. And boys. The kids were standing on either side of her, acting as walking sticks. She'd arranged the cashmere throw like a sarong, tucking it into itself so it hung from just above her breasts. Her curls were cascading in a tumbled mess around her shoulders.

She looked…fabulous, he thought, so suddenly that he felt a jab of what might even be described as heart pain. Or heart panic?

Two deep breaths. Professional. She was a patient. Nothing more.

He'd been over the idea of heart pain a long time ago.

'Hey, welcome to the world of up,' he said, and managed a smile he hoped was detached and clinically appropriate. 'I hope you're not weight bearing on that foot.'

'I have two great crutches,' she said, and smiled. 'One called Nathan and one called Martin.'

'Great job, boys,' he said, and nodded, and both little boys flushed with pleasure. Which gave him another jolt. It was hard to get these kids to smile.

Dammit, why had he forgotten the buns?

'Are they ready yet?' Martin asked, almost as the thought entered his head.

'Easter buns are for this afternoon,' he said, and he knew he sounded desperate.

'You said we could have them for breakfast,' Nathan said. 'The kids at school say they eat buns on Good Friday morning.'

'I've been eating them all week,' Erin chipped in, and he cast her a look that he hoped put her right back in her place. Talk about helpful… Not.

'Dom says Easter buns are for Easter and not before,' Martin told her. 'Like Easter eggs. He says if the bunny sees us eat an egg before Sunday he'll know he doesn't have to deliver eggs to our place.'

'So if he sees you eat a bun before this morning you won't get any?' Erin ventured, eyeing Dom with caution. 'Your dad's a stickler for rules, then.'

'Rules are good,' Martin said, though he sounded doubtful.

'They are good,' Erin agreed. 'As long as there aren't inter-

ruptions, like dogs having puppies and ladies crashing their car
to take a man's mind off his baking.'

'Actually, the buns flopped before...' Dom started, but Erin
shook her head.

'One good deed deserves another,' she said, smiling at him
from the doorway with a smile that said she knew exactly how
disconcerted he was. 'You're starting another batch now?'

'I started an hour ago but the instructions say it takes five hours.'

'At least,' she said. 'So your buns will have to be Buns
Batch Two.'

'Pardon?'

'Do you have self-raising flour?'

'Um...yes.'

'Butter?'

'Yes.'

'And dried fruit, of course?'

'Yes. Look, you can't—'

'Do very much at all,' she agreed cheerfully. 'Marilyn and her
puppies are asleep. There's no job for me there. I'm just hanging
around at a loose end in my very fetching sarong. But my foot
does hurt. So what say you give me a chair and a bowl and all
the ingredients I listed—oh, and milk. I need milk. And turn your
oven to as hot as you can make it. In twenty minutes I guarantee you'll have hot cross buns for breakfast.'

They did. True to her word, twenty minutes later they were
wrapping themselves round absolutely delicious hot cross buns.

Or, to be more specific, hot cross scones, Dom conceded as
he lathered butter onto his third. But who was nit-picking? He
surely wasn't. Neither were the boys. As per Erin's instructions,
they'd helped rub butter into the flour and helped her cut scones
from the dough. They'd painted on glaze to make crosses, using
sugar and egg white. They'd stood with their noses practically
pressed against the glass oven door as the scones...buns!...rose

in truly spectacular fashion. And now they were lining up for their third as well.

As was Erin. She was eating like she hadn't eaten for a week. He thought back to the retching of the night before. She was running on empty. He should have given her something…

'I wouldn't have been able to eat even if you'd offered,' she said, and his gaze jerked to meets hers.

'How did you know I was going to say—?'

'I could see it,' she said, wiping a daub of melted butter from her chin. 'You had that look my intern gets when he forgets to take some really minor part of a patient history. Like how many legs my patient has.'

'Like…'

'I came on duty one morning a few weeks back,' she continued, placidly reaching for another scone. 'According to my intern's notes, a patient who'd come in during the night was suffering from tingling in his legs. That was all it said. The nurses had set a cradle from his hips down so I couldn't see. I chatted to the patient for a couple of minutes, then asked if he could wriggle his toes.'

'And?' She had him fascinated.

'And he'd lost both legs in a motorbike accident twenty years ago,' she said, glowering, obviously remembering a Very Embarrassing Moment. 'He'd come in because he was getting weird tingling in his stumps and a bit of left-sided numbness. It transpired he'd had too much to drink, gone to sleep on a hard floor, then woken and panicked. I figured it out, but not before the students who were following me on my rounds did the world's biggest snigger.'

'So the look I had on my face just then…'

'Yep. It was like my intern looked when I came out of the ward and asked why a small matter like lack of legs wasn't in the patient notes. Last night all you did was not offer me a three-course meal when I was still queasy. So you can stop beating yourself up and pass me the jam.'

'Yes, ma'am,' he said faintly. 'These are great s...buns.'

'They are, aren't they?' she said smugly. 'I taught myself from the Australian Countrywomen's Association Cookbook, circa 1978.'

'Your mother didn't teach you?'

'No,' she said shortly, and a shadow crossed her face.

'Um...your mother...' he started.

'What about my mother?'

'Will she have hot cross buns waiting for your arrival?'

'Probably. Designer buns, though,' she said. 'She'll have ordered them from the most exclusive and expensive baker in Melbourne. She'll have unsalted butter imported from Denmark. If she wasn't staying at Charles's parents' place she'd be serving them on china that cost more than my weekly salary per piece, but Marjory will be making up for that. Marjory has exquisite porcelain all her own.'

'Marjory?'

'Charles's mother,' she said, and bit into her scone with a savagery that made him blink.

'Um...'

'Don't ask,' she said. 'I love them but they drive me nuts. In a while I'll phone and ask them to come and get me.' She looked down at her sarong and winced. 'I'm not sure what they'll think of my fashion sense. What do you think, boys?'

The little boys had been staring at her like she had two heads. They were totally entranced.

'It's very...nice,' Martin tried.

'My mum wore a blanket sometimes,' Nathan offered.

'Your mum...'

'I've washed your clothes,' Dom said, thinking maybe now was a good time to deflect the conversation. 'I put them in the washer last night—they're in the drier now. I'd expect you'll have decent clothes in about half an hour.'

'I think I ripped them.'

'You may have,' he agreed. 'Did you have any more? In the car?'

'Of course.'

'I let the police know about the crash last night. If the local cop doesn't arrive with your gear, we'll go and get it.'

'Did you really crash your car?' Martin asked.

'I did.' Then, seeing the boys' desire for gory detail, she relented. 'Marilyn, the dog, was in the middle of the road. I swerved to avoid hitting her. My car went off the road and rolled all the way down to the river.

'Rolled…' Nathan breathed.

'Rolled,' she agreed. 'Over and over. It was lucky I was wearing a seat belt or I'd have been squashed.'

'You must have been scared,' Martin said.

'I was.' She nodded, looking satisfactorily ghoulish. 'I could have been deader than a duck.' Her dark eyes twinkled. 'If it was a dead duck, that is.'

But Martin wasn't to be deflected. He was off in his own horror story. 'You might have rolled into the river and drowned,' he said, and frowned. 'I think my dad drowned. My aunty said he drowned himself in booze.'

'I'm so sorry,' Erin said, focusing directly on the little boy before her. Her playacting disappeared. Her expression was suddenly adult to adult, and Dom thought, This woman is skilled. Empathic. Kind. Her whole body language said she cared.

'I can't even remember him,' Martin said. 'I can remember Mum but she's gone, too.'

'Does that make you really sad?' Erin asked. Cautious.

'No, 'cos Dom's looking after me,' Martin said, cheering up. 'And Tansy, but Tansy's not here. But you're here, and now Marilyn is, too.'

'The dog's here only till this lady goes home,' Dom said warningly and Erin thought…

'No,' Dom said.

She looked startled. 'What?'

'It's two who can play at face-reading,' he retorted. 'I'm

sorry you crashed your car. I'm also very sorry for Marilyn but I can't keep her.'

'You can't...' She paused. 'No. I... Of course you can't.'

'I'm looking after two boys and the medical needs of this entire community,' he said. 'Normally I have a housekeeper...'

'No wife?' she said before she could stop herself.

'No wife,' he agreed, and smiled at her evident confusion. 'I'm sorry. Last night you assumed there was, and because you were scared it seemed more sensible to let you believe it. We normally have a live-in housekeeper—Tansy. She's great, isn't she, boys? But her sister had a baby last week so Tansy's flown to Queensland to help out. Which means when I get an urgent callout the boys have to come with me. I can hardly take Marilyn and the pups as well. I can only take on so much.'

'Of course you can,' she said, hurriedly. 'I...I'll think of something.'

'Of course you will,' he said, and had to bite back the urge to say, Stay here. Of course we can keep your dog. We can keep you, too, if you want.

Which was ridiculous. There was no earthly reason why he should look at this woman and feel his heart hammer in his chest. She was a patient, who'd come to him for help.

She didn't belong here.

His body was telling him she did.

His body had better go take a hike.

Maybe he had more of his mother in him than he thought. His mother had believed in love at first sight and she'd messed with both of their lives because of it. Her romantic ideals had turned into loser after loser. She saw life through rose-coloured glasses, and her dreams turned to nightmares every time.

'I have work to do,' he said abruptly.

'I won't interfere.'

'I know you won't,' he said. And added silently as he left, for his ears only, Because I won't let you.

* * *

She'd upset him. He'd walked out of the room like he couldn't leave fast enough. Like she was contagious.

Ridiculous. She must be mistaken.

She ate another scone and had a second cup of coffee and talked to the boys. The tumble-drier whirred to a halt in the next room, and Dom appeared again, with an armful of clean, dry clothes.

'Do you want to phone your family?' he asked, brusque and businesslike. 'You lost your cellphone, didn't you. You can use my land line.'

She glanced at her watch. Nine. If she was driving from Melbourne this morning she'd hardly arrive before eleven. They wouldn't be worrying. She could have a couple more hours…

Of what? Sitting in this man's kitchen eating more hot cross scones while he stayed out of her way?

Stupid. She was avoiding the inevitable. She had to go.

And Marilyn? If she was careful she could get her onto the back seat of Charles's or her father's car, she decided. Sure, they shouldn't disrupt her but it was a whole lot better than putting her down. Which was the alternative.

'You could ring the local animal shelter,' Dom said, watching her face and seeing her indecision. 'They might be able to do something.'

'On the first day of a four-day holiday? An injured stray with hours-old puppies?' She shook her head. 'I'll think of something.' She rose to her feet. Feeling shaky. Feeling unaccountably desolate.

'I'll fetch some crutches from the surgery.'

'Thank you.'

'We can be your crutches,' Martin said stoically. But he was looking doubtful. 'Are you taking the puppies away?'

'They're Erin's puppies,' Dom said.

'Does she want them?' Martin looked at Erin with eyes that said he'd been lied to in the past. His clear, green eyes were challenging.

'Of course I want them,' Erin said, forcing brightness. And then she glanced out into the hall and saw the heap of doggie content-ment by the door. 'Of course I want them,' she reiterated, sounding more sure of herself. 'It's just a matter of convincing my family.'

Her family en masse—including Charles's parents—were appalled. Erin tried to downplay the accident—a skid on a wet road to avoid a dog—but for her extended family, even a minor incident had the power to dredge up fearsome memories. It took a while to assure her mother she wasn't hurt, honest, it had been a minor accident, and, no, she didn't need their help, she only needed someone to fetch her.

Her mother put Charles on. So Charles hadn't told them what had happened between them? Or maybe he had but he'd ex-plained she was being silly. Hormonal, he'd said the last time she'd seen him, which had made her want to hit him.

By the time she spoke to Charles she was emotionally wrung out. She didn't have energy left to explain she still had Marilyn.

'I'll be there as soon as I can,' Charles said, and she knew she'd shaken him as well. She knew he'd come fast.

She didn't want Charles. She wanted her dad to come, but of course they acted as a team.

They all cared for her. They cared for her so well she felt…stifled.

The doorbell pealed while she was getting dressed and her feeling of oppression deepened. But then she thought, surely Charles couldn't be here already.

Maybe it was another patient. Maybe it was another need for Dom to face this Easter.

If he was called out… Maybe she could stay with the boys for a while, she thought. As a thank-you gesture. Charles wouldn't mind waiting. He could have one of her hot cross scones.

She hauled her windcheater over her head and opened the living-room door with caution. Dom was at the front door, facing a stranger.

The man in the doorway was long, lanky and unkempt. He was maybe six feet four or so. He had limp, dirty hair that hung in dreadlocks to his shoulders. He was wearing tattered clothes and frayed sandals, and in his hands he was holding the biggest Easter egg Erin had ever seen. As big as two footballs, the thing was wider than he was.

'I'm here to see Nathan,' the man snapped, and then started coughing. Dom took the egg and waited until the coughing ceased.

'Nathan,' he called down the passage.

Marilyn was right behind him in the hall, between Erin and the front door, between Dom and Erin. As he glanced backward past the dog, Dom's eyes met Erin's. He gave her a blank stare— the sort of look doctors gave each other in the emergency department to say caution, act with care.

Nathan came running out of the kitchen. He saw who was at the front door—and stopped.

'Here's your dad,' Dom said, gently, Erin noticed. 'I think he's brought you a present.

'I can tell my kid that myself,' the man said, aggressively.

'Would you like to come in?' Dom asked. He gestured to Marilyn. 'Sorry about the mess. Our dog gave birth to puppies last night in just the wrong place.'

Our dog? Okay, maybe anything else would be too hard to explain, Erin conceded. For now Marilyn was communal property.

'I'm not coming in,' the man growled. 'This place gives me the creeps.'

'It's a safe house, Dad,' Nathan said in a small voice. 'No one hits you here.'

There was moment's deathly silence. The man seemed to freeze.

'No one hits you anywhere,' the man said finally, in a voice that said he didn't believe it himself.

No one responded.

'How's the methadone programme going?' Dom asked, and the man's anger returned.

'Bloody stuff doesn't work. You know that.'

'So you're using again?'

'Yeah, but I want the kid.'

'You know the courts said you need to be clear for three months before they'll consider it. Methadone and testing—you know the drill. We've been through it over and over. People are trying to help you.'

'F…do-gooders.'

'It's all we can do, Michael,' Dom said wearily. 'Would you like some breakfast?'

'Nah. I just want to give the kid the egg.' He held it toward Nathan, not moving an inch inside the house. 'Come on, Nathe,' he said in a wheedling voice. 'I bought it good and proper. With me pension money.'

'It's pretty big,' Nathan said, but he didn't look pleased. In fact, he looked close to tears.

'So come and get it,' Michael said.

Nathan edged forward along the hallway, inching his way past Marilyn. But it wasn't the dog he was scared of, Erin thought. When he reached Michael his face was bleached white. Dom's hand came down to rest on his shoulder.

'Hey, it's good that your dad's brought you an egg,' he said.

'Y-yeah.' Nathan took a deep breath, as if searching for courage. He reached out and the egg was shoved into his arms.

'There,' Michael said, satisfied. 'You can't say I don't have contact with him. Can you?' he demanded of Dom belligerently.

'Of course I can't,' Dom said. 'But if you want custody you need to get serious about the methadone programme.'

'Yeah, yeah. After Easter. When I get me life in order a bit. But me and a mate are going surfing.' He glanced out to the street where an ancient purple kombi van was clearly waiting for him. 'I'd love to take you, Nathe.'

'Yes,' Nathan said, but his hand crept into Dom's and held it.

The man noticed. His face darkened with anger. 'Why, you little…'

'Nathan's had flu,' Dom said quickly as the man's hand raised. 'He's had almost a week off school.'

It was enough to deflect Michael. His hand paused.

'My kid's been sick? Why didn't you tell me?'

'I left a message at your boarding house.'

'I haven't been there for weeks.' Out on the street whoever was driving the van was clearly getting impatient. There was a long, loud blast of the horn.

'I hope the surf's great,' Dom said neutrally, and Michael cast him an uncertain look—deciding, Erin thought, whether to stoke his anger or not. And finally, blessedly, deciding not.

'Yeah, it will be,' he said at last. 'I gotta go. But, Nathe, remember I gave you the egg. I do what I can. Love ya, mate.' And he wheeled away and half ran back to the van. Leaving Nathan clutching Dominic's hand.

This was none of her business. She should go back into her sitting cum bedroom. But she was too interested to retreat.

Dom and Nathan stayed with their backs to her, watching the van disappear. Nathan didn't release Dominic's hand. When finally the sound of the van retreated to silence he glanced up at Dom and his small face was a mess of tears. 'The Easter Bunny won't come now.'

'Yeah, he will,' Dom said, placid in the face of the little boy's distress. 'You know the rules. If the Easter Bunny sees you eating an egg before Sunday he knows he doesn't need to deliver eggs. But lots of people give eggs before Sunday. Three of my patients left me eggs and they're sitting on my desk right now. I just have to be very good and not eat them.'

'So I can't eat Dad's egg?'

'Not until Sunday. Not if you want the bunny to come,' Dom said, with all the gravity in the world.

He was great, Erin thought.

He was…gorgeous?

Um…what? Where had that come from? Gorgeous? Hardly appropriate.

Or, actually, incredibly appropriate. The man's kindness made her blink back tears. Sexy came in all forms. Sexy came in the guise of a guy holding a little boy by the hand and discussing the Easter Bunny with the same gravity he might accord World Peace.

'I guess,' Nathan was saying, still doubtful.

'It's true. All you need do is put it with the others that we'll eat after Easter.'

'Okay,' Nathan said, his face finally clearing as he decided to believe. Then he added, 'I'm glad he's gone. Will he come back soon?'

'I don't know, Nathe,' Dom admitted, and the little boy's face clouded.

'He might,' he whispered. But then the clouds disappeared again. 'But he said he was going surfing for Easter and that's days and days. He won't come back till after the Easter bunny's been. I'll tell Martin.'

And he handed his egg to Dom, edged past the bundle of canine contentment on the floor and scooted off to find his…brother?

She didn't think so. A few assumptions were being stood on their heads this morning.

Dom was standing in the hallway holding the egg. It really was ridiculously large.

Marilyn snoozed at his feet, with her three puppies. Erin could hear Nathan talking to Martin back in the kitchen.

How many responsibilities did this man have?

'The boys are your…foster-kids?' she ventured, and he nodded. He was watching her, an expression on his face like he couldn't figure her out.

'What?' she said.

He shook his head as if clearing fog. 'Nothing,' he said. 'Um…yeah, they're my foster-kids.'

'But you don't have a wife.'

'You don't need a wife to foster kids.'

'I thought…'

'If I wanted to adopt a cute baby with no strings attached then, yeah, I'd need to be married. I'd need references practically from the Pope himself. But I take kids when there's a problem—a reason they need closer supervision than even foster-parents can give. If I'm willing to take a kid like Martin, whose mother's disappeared but who might surface at any minute, in any state, or Nathan, whose dad is…well, like you saw him, then there's not so much competition that you'd notice. References from the Pope might be waived.'

'But you're a doctor. Part time?' she ventured.

'In this town? Full time and part time as well.' Then, as her confusion became obvious, he added, 'It's manageable. I have a great housekeeper and the boys come with me a lot. They come here traumatised, caught up in their own dysfunctional worlds. With me they see lots of other worlds, many of them just as dysfunctional, but I give them a solid base. I give them rules and I give them a hug when they need one.'

He broke off as the doorbell pealed again. Nathan's head emerged from the kitchen, looking fearful.

'It's okay, Nathe,' he said. 'Hop it. I'll deal with it.'

Nathan disappeared. Dom tugged the door wide.

It was Charles. Six feet two, blond and tanned, wearing cream chinos, a quality linen shirt with top buttons casually unfastened, and soft leather boat shoes. He really was absurdly handsome, Erin thought. Behind him, in the driveway, was his Porsche. Sleek and handsome as he was.

Charles was a general physician whose patients numbered some of the wealthiest people in Melbourne. He knew what he wanted in life, did Charles, and he didn't like hiccups.

What was happening now was clearly a hiccup, and it was the second hiccup in a week. The first had been on Tuesday when she'd knocked back his very reasonable request to marry him.

'Erin.' He looked straight past Dominic, seeing only her. His glance took her in, from her bare toes to her hair, still tangled and wet from the shower. 'My God. You said you weren't hurt. The crutches...'

'I cut my foot,' she said, and managed a smile. 'Lots of little scratches. They'll heal fast and I already look a lot better than I did last night. Charles, this is Dr Dominic Spencer. He came to my rescue.'

'I'm very grateful,' Charles said, and gripped Dom's hand in what Erin knew would be an exceedingly manly handshake. 'Not that there was any need. If she'd just phoned...'

He was grateful. As if he owned her. What more did she have to say to cut herself loose? 'I told you,' she explained, when he turned on his reproachful look on her. 'I lost my cellphone, and by the time I got here it was three in the morning. I didn't want to worry Mum and Dad.'

'They're worried now,' Charles said, reproving. 'Crashing the car—for a dog. Honestly, Erin, you know not to swerve for animals. You know better than most what tragedy crashes can cause. But I won't say anything. If you're ready, we'll leave. We'll take a look at your car on the way, see what we can salvage and ring the insurance people before we do anything. That car's practically new. I don't want it looted.'

I don't want it looted. The proprietary thing was automatic.

She should never have let it get this far, she thought bleakly. But it had happened so gradually she hadn't noticed. According to Charles, her parents had always assumed they'd marry. His parents had always assumed they'd marry. So had Charles.

It was only when he'd suggested they break the news to the parents this Easter and maybe take a family excursion to buy the ring that she'd realised how far those assumptions had gone.

Was marriage supposed to be like this? An assumption that it'd be good for all concerned?

So on Tuesday she'd tried to explain it but he'd simply smiled at her like an avuncular big brother 'it's only nerves. It's okay. Come home at Easter and we'll discuss it.'

She so nearly hadn't come. But her parents were already staying with Charles's parents. They'd been planning this Easter for months. They'd all be so upset…

Charles was smiling at her. Waiting for an answer. Ready to start his very reasonable discussion again.

Dom was watching from the sidelines.

'It'll hardly be looted where it is,' Erin managed. 'And…um…Charles, there's also the problem of Marilyn.'

'Marilyn?'

'The…my dog.' She gestured to Marilyn on the floor behind her. 'She was the one on the road last night. I'm keeping her.'

Charles glanced at the dog. And then glanced again. In horror.

Marilyn was rousing. Her intravenous line had provided her with fluids, antibiotics and pain relief. Her puppies had drunk their fill and were now sleeping.

With a weary heave, she stumbled to her feet. Dom had left a water bowl by her side. She inspected it with caution, looked up at the three humans watching her and then lowered her head to drink.

Erin found she was grinning. She glanced at Dom and he was grinning, too.

'I'll take the IV line out,' Dom said, sounding exceedingly satisfied. 'She'll want to go outside.'

'What,' Charles said, in a voice that said he didn't believe what he was seeing, 'is that?'

'It's the dog I was telling you about,' Erin explained patiently. 'She had puppies last night. And I'm keeping her,' she repeated. 'I'm keeping them all.'

Ignoring them, Dom dropped to his knees. While Marilyn drank he slipped the IV line out, putting pressure on the entry point for a moment with a wad of clean tissues he tugged from his pocket. What sort of a man carried an excess supply of tissues? Erin wondered.

A guy who was used to life's messes.

A really sexy doctor who was used to life's messes.

'That's great,' Dom said cheerfully, as Marilyn kept on drinking. 'I'm thinking she'll settle, wherever you take her. She was great this morning while I cleaned her side—she's a lovely, placid pooch. You'll have to give the rest of the antibiotic orally but she should be fine.'

'You'll have to give...' Charles repeated faintly, and stared at Erin in horror. 'You're kidding.'

'I'm not kidding,' Erin said solidly. 'I can't leave her here.'

'Why not?'

'Dom has enough on his plate. He has kids.'

'Kids like dogs,' Charles said flatly. 'I can't believe this. You crashed the car for *this*?'

'Hey,' Dom said. 'Mind the insults. You need to be wary of new mothers. Very hormonal.'

He was still grinning. Laughing at…Charles? At her situation? Erin turned a shoulder to tell him what she thought of that—and tried to concentrate on Charles. 'I have to take her.'

'Not to my parents', you can't,' Charles said bluntly. 'Mum'd have kittens.'

'That'd add to the menagerie,' Dom said, still grinning.

'Your mother would have forty fits as well,' Charles added. 'And I can't imagine how Peppy would react.'

'Who's Peppy?' Dom asked, interested. 'Great Aunt Peppy?'

'Peppy's my mother's poodle,' Erin snapped. She could do without the levity.

'Your parents and Charles's parents live together?'

'We're having a family Easter,' Erin said, trying not to sound…strained. Knowing she hadn't pulled it off. 'Our parents are old friends. Charles's parents asked us all for Easter.'

'That's great,' Dom said, and suddenly the laughter was gone. His tone had turned implacable. 'That's six adults to look after one dog and three pups. Two dogs if you count Peppy.' Behind him, his phone started ringing. 'Can you excuse me? I need to answer this.' Then he glanced at Marilyn who was looking—meaningfully—at the door. 'Could you guys take Marilyn out to the garden? Now she's off her IV line, I'm thinking she might need a walk.' He carried his phone into the kitchen and closed the door.

Walk. Right. Not so much a walk as a stagger, Erin thought. For both of them.

She ignored Charles for the moment—she was taking Marilyn and there was nothing she could do to help him come to terms with the inevitable. Dom's wellingtons were at the door—used, she guessed, for carting wood in the rain or something equally bucolic and messy. This was where she was now, she thought ruefully. Country and messy. She hauled on the boots over her dressings, and then—as Charles still didn't move—she limped to the stairs. Marilyn followed.

They struggled, but both of them made it down the couple of shallow steps and onto the grass. Marilyn sniffed the grass in appreciation, cast Erin a look of what seemed to be gratitude and did what was expected.

Last night in the dark and confusion and fear Erin had thought the dog was fat. Now she saw the too-prominent ribs, the sunken face. The legs that trembled. But the terror of the night was over. Marilyn turned her big, ugly face up to the morning sun as if soaking in its warmth. Erin gazed down and felt her heart wobble.

Last night it had seemed as if the world was ending—for her as well as for Marilyn. Last night, as the car had rolled, for a long terrifying moment she'd thought she might die. Marilyn had been close to death. This morning the sun was glinting on the sea, on both of their faces, on their lives, and here they were, ready to start again.

For this dog, life was about to change. It must, no matter what.

Even if her own life changed in the process. For that was how she felt right now. It was as if she'd never felt the sun on her face before. Like she'd woken from a dream and found a new reality.

Maybe she was being dumb. Fanciful. But she looked down at Marilyn and her resolution was absolute. Knocking Charles's proposal back was only the start of it.

'Hey,' she said softly, and squatted on her heels in the soft grass. It hurt a bit but her foot was nothing compared with what Marilyn had been through. 'You're a dog in a million.'

'She's not,' Charles said from the veranda. He'd made no move to help. He seemed too…stunned. 'Erin, get serious. If this guy…'

'You mean Dominic.'

'If this guy can't take her…'

'He can't. He's the only doctor for the town and he's a single dad.'

'Then she has to be put down,' Charles went on, inexorably. 'You know that. She's a stray. No one wants her.'

'Do you mind?' She put her hands over Marilyn's ears. 'Do you know what she's been through? Someone threw her out of their car.'

'All the more reason to do what's sensible,' he said, and then softened his tone. 'Sweetheart, I know you've had a rotten shock. If this guy can't take the dog…'

'I'm not your sweetheart.'

'And I can't take the dog.' Dominic was abruptly with them again, pushing the screen door wide with a bang and striding down the steps with speed. 'Sorry, but I need to go. I've called a neighbour to come over and care for the boys but I can't wait. I've had a call—a kid with nut allergy. Jamie's gone into anaphylactic shock. They're driving him to meet me. Can you stay with the boys until Dulcie gets here?' He was heading for the garage at a run. 'Great to meet you both. See you again some time.'

Anaphylactic shock…

Erin's mind switched into medical mode, just like that. If a child's reaction was severe…

This was what she did.

Without making a conscious decision, she found herself running, not noticing her feet, reaching Dom's car almost as he did.

'I'm going, too,' she yelled over her shoulder to Charles. 'Can you look after Marilyn? And the two kids inside.' She slid into the passenger seat.

Dom paused, hand on the ignition. 'What the hell…?'

'You might need help. Go.'

'Charles—'

'He's a doctor, too. He understands emergencies. I'm an accident and emergency specialist. I can help. Go, Dominic. Move.'

CHAPTER FOUR

HE HAD help.

He shouldn't have let her come. She was hurt herself. He glanced across at her but she stared straight ahead, her face determined. Like she thought he was going to stop the car and kick her out.

He didn't have time to argue. But even if he wanted to…

She was another doctor.

Last night he'd had insight into this woman's medical skills. Maybe it could make the difference in whether Jamie Sutherland lived or died.

Okay, he wasn't about to argue.

He had his phone in the car cradle now. He phoned the ambulance in Campbelltown, requesting help. Then he concentrated on driving. Concentrated on what lay ahead.

'Tell me what we're facing,' Erin said into the silence. He was speeding as fast as he dared without putting themselves in danger, but his foot on the accelerator must tell its own story. She knew this was life or death.

'Jamie's eight years old. He's had a couple of near misses. Last time it was from a friend's mum making peanut-butter sandwiches, not washing the knife and then making him a ham sandwich. He nearly died. This time he's eaten half a muesli bar. His cousin told him it didn't have nuts in. It's chock full of 'em.'

'His parents have what they need?'

'They have adrenaline, antihistamine and an action plan. They've done everything they can, but they phoned from the car and I could hear him choking.'

'You wasted time ringing the neighbour.'

'I don't have a choice,' he said grimly. 'Martin and Nathan aren't safe on their own.'

'I would have—'

'It was quicker to phone Dulcie rather than hope you'd do it.'

She fell silent. But he could sense what she was thinking.

'I don't know you,' he said at last. 'I couldn't trust that…'

'Of course you couldn't.' She shook her head, as if convincing herself, obviously trying to see the whole picture. 'But…if Martin and Nathan need such close supervision…if you're the only doctor for miles…is it fair that you take on their care?'

'Of course it's not.'

She blinked. 'Sorry. But…'

'But nothing. Of course it's not fair,' he repeated, savagely. 'They need a full-time carer. But they've both come from such appalling backgrounds that no foster-family will take them. You get Nathan, you get Michael in your life as well, and he's dangerous. Martin's mother is just plain weird. She only loves Martin when he's sick so she tries to make him sick. It's Munchausen's by proxy syndrome. He gets sick or is hurt, she gets sympathy and attention. Martin's starting to believe the way to affection is self-harm. Dreadful stuff. So these kids stay with me or they go into juvenile detention because there's nowhere else secure enough for them to go.'

'You'd take on these people…'

'If I have to. To protect my kids.'

'That's crazy.'

'Yeah,' he said, and he thought, *She's right. It's crazy. Why the hell did he do it?*

* * *

He's crazy, she thought. Nuts.

Dom was focused again on his driving, on the road ahead, on getting to where they had to be without killing them both.

She'd never met such single-minded purpose.

He was... He was...

Um...no. Back in your box, she told herself, feeling weirdly off key.

She'd been off key all week. She hadn't realised how close Charles was to proposing—she hadn't figured how much their parents were depending on it. These last few days had been shock enough without falling for...falling for...

Whoa. No!

I must have hit my head last night, she thought. Everything before now seemed out of focus. Unimportant.

What was important was Dom.

She could help him.

'Will you quit it with the staring?' he said, and she caught herself.

'Sorry. I was thinking...'

Thinking what? What should she be thinking?

Work. Of what lay before them. Of course. 'How equipped are you?'

'I can do surgery in the middle of the road if I need to, and I might just need to,' he said grimly. 'We nearly lost him last time.' Then he visibly braced himself, and she could see he was slipping into a mode where he could work. She'd seen surgeons do this before a dicey operation. Push away the negatives. Go in full of confidence, even if their hearts should be in their boots. 'But, hey, it's daylight so I don't need lights. I have the gear I need and another doctor with me—even if her footwear does leave a bit to be desired. Who needs theatres and theatre staff?'

Then, as if on cue, another car came into view. It had to be the people they were meeting, Erin thought. The car came over the hump of the hill at such high speed the rear appeared airborne.

Dom pulled off the road, fast. Well off. The Sutherlands' car was beside them in seconds, brakes screeching, a cloud of black smoke and burnt rubber left in its wake as it skidded dangerously onto the verge. Dom was out of his car and pulling open the back door of their car almost before it stopped. Erin followed. And saw their patient.

On the back seat, cradled in his mother's arms, lay a child, limp and blue—desperately ill. Erin only caught a fleeting glimpse—enough to make her catch her breath in dismay—before Dom was blocking her view.

She wasn't here to look. She was here to work. Dom had his medical case on the back seat of his car. She hauled it out, laid it on the grass and tugged it open. Searching for what she needed. Seconds later Dom was laying the little boy down beside her. His hand was on Jamie's neck, trying to find a pulse.

'Yes,' he said.

So there was hope. If there was still a pulse… A little air must have been getting through until now.

But no longer.

The child's face was swollen. His mouth was open as if he'd been gasping for breath. Even without putting her fingers in his mouth—as Dom was doing now—she could see his tongue was so swollen his airway must be blocked.

His chest didn't move.

'Trache,' she said into the stillness, and Dom nodded. A tracheotomy was the only way they'd save him now.

'Scalpel and trache tube,' he snapped.

That was what she was here for. She had what he needed out of the case, ready, before he finished the words, and was tugging a swab package open with her teeth.

Dom felt the little boy's throat, slowing a little, acting with care. The need was urgent but not urgent enough to risk cutting in the wrong place.

Erin's fingers held the swab, waiting for Dom to lift his hand. Behind her, Jamie's mother started sobbing. His dad had sunk to his knees on the verge and was pleading simply, over and over, 'Please, please, please.'

How many tracheotomies had Dom performed? She'd done them but, then, Dom only had her word that she was who she said she was. This was no time to verify her credentials.

If Dom had looked unsure she'd offer, but Dom's bearing was of grim intent, a man who knew what had to be done and wasn't about to hesitate—or offer the procedure to someone he didn't know—when hesitancy could mean Jamie's life.

So she swabbed. She set her hands on the sides of Jamie's head, making sure he kept motionless.

And Dom didn't falter. He made a small, neat slit in the central neck, down to the trachea. Into the trachea.

He pressed the tube in—and the thing was done.

But this was no guarantee of life. Jamie's body was shutting down. It had been two minutes, maybe three, since they'd arrived and she hadn't seen any sign of breathing. He'd ceased struggling.

Dom leaned over and blew gently into the airway. Again.

And then, magically, Jamie's chest heaved all on its own. Air sucked into the tube without Dom's help, sucked involuntarily by lungs that knew what they needed.

Again.

And then the little boy's eyes fluttered wide. He stared up at Dom in confusion, and the start of panic.

Dom tightened his hold so the airway couldn't shift out of position. 'Hey, Jamie,' he said, firmly, surely. 'It's okay, mate. You ate something with peanuts in it, and your throat's swollen. We've popped in a tube to help you breathe. It's important to keep still until we get the swelling down.'

This was one smart little boy. And brave. He stared up at Dom, and Erin saw recognition; she saw the moment when he decided to trust.

He breathed on. All by himself. His chest rose and fell. Rose and fell.

He'd live.

She felt tears well behind her eyes. Unprofessional? Maybe. She didn't care.

'Here's your mum and dad,' Dom said, keeping his voice calm and prosaic, still holding Jamie tight. He raised his voice a notch, talking to the woman behind him. 'Casey, Jamie's breathing again. Your crying is scaring him. Rob, can you tell your son he's going to be fine?'

It was a command, no matter how softly spoken, and Jamie's bravery must be inherited. Jamie's parents were themselves again in moments.

Casey brushed tears fiercely away from her face. She knelt beside Jamie and took his hand.

'No cuddling yet,' Dom said, but he was smiling. 'Let's keep Jamie nice and still until his breathing's settled. You injected the adrenaline pen at home okay? Great. I know, it didn't work as well as we hoped, but it gave us time. Erin, can you prepare a syringe with light sedation?'

'Are you a nurse?' Casey asked her, her eyes not leaving her son's face.

'This is Dr Carmody,' Dom said, answering for her. 'She's not like the doctors you've met before, eh? Wellingtons must be the latest fashion for lady doctors. Do you reckon they'll take over from white coats? They're about as sexy, don't you think?'

It was light banter, Erin thought. Dom was talking them all down from horror.

Herself included.

She was used to emergencies. Emergencies were what she did for a living. But even in her city emergency department, a case such as this, where a child had come so close to death, would shake her to the core.

She still needed to be professional. She did not need to cry. She never cried at work. Why the sudden urge now?

Emotions. Hormones. Her world was shifting.

Stupid. Fanciful. Undeniable.

Jamie breathed on while Erin administered light sedation. She did it without conferring but Dom watched her; watched the dose. She felt on trial. A new kid in school, desperate to please the big guy.

Or not. It was a fanciful way of thinking. She was here to help, not to think about what Dom was thinking about her.

Or to cry.

Stupid, stupid, stupid.

And then, at last, the ambulance arrived. Two skilled paramedics took over. They knew Dom well. She could see they respected him. As well they might, she thought.

Jamie would need to spend the night in hospital, until the swelling subsided. 'There's no hospital here,' Dom told her, regretful. 'We have a small one but with only one doctor we had to close it. There's a paediatrician in Campbelltown. Jamie will be in good hands.'

They loaded Jamie into the ambulance. His mother went with him.

His dad followed behind, driving the family car.

Dom and Erin were left alone, standing on the verge of a country road, with the debris of an emergency around them.

She still wanted to cry.

'Let's get you home,' Dom said gently, and she made a last-ditch attempt to get herself together. And found suddenly there was a wad of tissues in her hand.

'I'm n-not c-crying,' she stammered. 'I never cry.'

'I can see that,' he said, and he wasn't smiling.

'It's just…'

'You had a really big night last night.' He paused. 'Thank you,' he said softly.

'Thank…me?'

'You know we only had seconds. The seconds you gave me here may well have made the difference. Thank you for being here.'

'It's my pleasure,' Erin said, and subsided under her tissues, trying not to wail. 'It's all my pleasure.'

Charles was waiting.

They didn't have to go into the house to find him. He was out on the road, standing beside his Porsche, looking angry.

'Uh-oh,' Erin said.

'You want a medical defence?' Dom pulled up behind the Porsche. He climbed out of the car before Erin could do the same.

'We saved a life,' he said, before Charles could speak. 'Erin was great.'

But Charles's expression didn't relax. Given time to think, to assess the crisis for what it was, he'd have offered to help himself. But being left behind to play nursery maid would have made him…well, like he was now.

'Did Dulcie come?' Dom asked.

'Yes,' he said shortly. 'She's in the house with the boys.'

'Thank you for helping out,' Dom said, and held out his hand.

It wasn't taken. Charles stared down at it like he didn't know what Dom was offering.

'I had to go, Charles,' Erin said, then thought, Damn, that had sounded like pleading and why should she plead?

'Of course you did,' Charles said, obviously making an effort to sound pleasant. 'So do we. Grab your things from the house, get rid of that footwear and we'll leave.'

'With Marilyn.'

Charles's attempt at a smile faded. 'You can't take the dog to my mother's house.'

'We won't stay on. I'll ask my parents to take us home.'

'You think your parents would let you keep the dog?'

'I'm not a kid.'

'Hey, why don't I go inside and make sure the kids are okay?' Dom interjected, looking mildly interested and nothing else—and Erin fought off a need to grab his arm and say stay.

She didn't. She was a big kid. She almost felt grown up.

'You're okay?' Dom asked, and that tiny gesture of caring suddenly had her feeling tears welling up again. What was wrong with her? She was turning into a wuss.

She sniffed. Loudly. 'I'm fine,' she managed, and he cast her a doubtful look and then nodded and headed for the house.

But when he reached the veranda he turned back. 'I can find someone to drive you back to Melbourne if you want,' he called.

Erin didn't answer. She couldn't trust herself to speak.

But Melbourne sounded good.

Marilyn aside, she didn't want to go placidly with Charles. She didn't want her parents—and Charles's parents—looking reproachfully at her, making her feel sorry for Charles, making her feel sorry for them.

She'd had over twenty years of sorry. Surely that was enough. Sorry was doing her head in.

'I mean it,' Dom said, and went inside and closed the door.

Erin closed her eyes. Actually…the way Dom was making her feel was doing her head in.

'Erin, what the hell's going on?' Charles said. 'You're behaving like a child.'

'I'm not.'

'Don't tell me—'

'No, don't tell me,' she snapped. 'Enough. I'm sorry you've all got the wrong idea. You're my friend, Charles, but you're not my lover. And while I love my parents—and I love your parents—and I even love you in a way, but not in the way you figure I should—I need to get on with my life. *My* life.'

He was staring at her like she'd suddenly turned green and sprouted horns. She must have been really wimpy up until now, she thought. Why had it taken so long to stand on her own two feet?

'It's this guy, isn't it?' he demanded. 'This is crazy.'

'It's not Dom. I only met him last night, and what I'm saying to you now has been coming for a while. Maybe it's about twenty years overdue.' She took a deep breath. 'Okay. Thank you for coming to get me, but I'm not coming with you. I need to figure myself out first. I'll ring Mum tonight. Meanwhile tell them I'm fine, but I was put up last night by a doctor who's the sole medical professional for fifty miles. I'd like to repay him by helping out with his kids and with his practice over Easter. If he doesn't want that, then I'll go back to Melbourne.'

'With him?' He said *him* like he was referring to some sort of pond scum.

'*He*…Dominic…offered to find someone to drive me to Melbourne. He didn't offer to drive me himself. There's nothing between us, Charles. How can there be?' She took a deep breath. 'But despite that…Dom's been wonderful. He's a…a…really wonderful doctor. I need to make the offer. If he wants me, I'm staying on.'

When she came back inside Dom was sitting in the kitchen munching on another of Erin's scones. The kids were waving goodbye to Dulcie from the back veranda. Dom glanced out the window and Charles's Porsche was disappearing down the road. What the hell…?

'He's gone without you,' he said, warily.

'You said there was someone who could drive me to Melbourne.' She hesitated. 'That is, if you don't want me to stay.'

He'd been about to take a bite of his scone. He didn't. 'Um… If I don't want you to stay?'

'I sort of thought I might be useful,' she said, sounding uncertain. 'Seeing Tansy's away. If there are more emergencies. If you want me to.'

'Is this because of the dog?'

She tilted her chin at that, a gesture he was starting to recognise. 'I have friends in Melbourne who'd take her in. For a few days at least until I'm sorted. But I'm offering to stay here for Easter. Only if you can use me, though. I won't stay unless I can be useful.'

She wanted to stay for Easter?

The thought took his breath away.

There were all sorts of reactions Dom ought to be feeling.

He ought to be furious she'd landed not only her dog but also herself in his care.

He ought to be wary. Charles's body language had been unmistakeably possesive. There was no way he wanted to be landed in a domestic dispute and this had the makings of a doozy.

He ought to be cautious about…well, about the way she was looking right now. She was a qualified doctor—a colleague—but she looked a waif. And then he thought, no. She was wearing torn jeans and a stained windcheater. She'd ditched his boots by the door and was wearing a pair of his too-big socks.

What she looked was really extraordinarily beautiful, but there was no room in his life for what he was thinking right now.

Except he was thinking it. What warm-blooded male could help but think it?

'So you won't kick me out?' she asked, and her eyes warmed, just a little. As if she guessed his thought.

How could she?

'You cook a mean hot cross scone,' he said, cautious.

'I can do all sorts of neat tricks,' she said. 'Mind, I'm a bit restricted.' She sat down and held up a socked foot. 'I think my dressing's coming off.'

'I'll re-dress it. Do you need a painkiller?'

'Yes,' she said promptly. 'Painkiller first. Then dressing.'

'You're telling me how to practise medicine?'

'I'm bossy,' she retorted, recovering spirit. 'You need to learn that about me. I plan to run a very efficient emergency department.'

'Run?'

'I accepted the top job last week.' She tried not to sound cocky—and failed. He had to smile.

'Where?'

'Melbourne East Emergency.'

'How old are you?' he demanded, astonished, and it was her turn to grin.

'How rude. Next you'll be asking about my love life.'

'I'm assuming your love life is currently driving off in a huff and a Porsche.'

'How insightful. Driving off into the sunset.' She sighed. 'Don't worry about it. I'm sure I'll make a great spinster. I'd planned to keep cats but now…maybe it's bulldogs.'

'You're serious?'

'Serious?'

'Your boyfriend's angry?'

'He is so not my boyfriend,' she said, and glowered. 'He sort of assumed he was—he assumed all sorts of things—and when I realised…' She shrugged. 'Sorry. This is not your problem.'

'So…' He wasn't sure where this was going. 'Your plan is?'

'To help you,' she said. 'If you admit you need help. Which, seeing you're male, might be difficult but if you try hard I'm thinking you might come round.'

She smiled.

Her smile was extraordinary.

This woman's life, whichever way he looked at it, was in turmoil. In the last twelve hours she'd almost died, she'd been thrown into someone else's Easter, she'd gained a dog and she seemed to have lost a perfectly good boyfriend. And yet she could still smile.

He was feeling…stunned, he thought. He was feeling like the wisest course was to get her out of here fast.

'You have a house in Melbourne?'

'I have a hospital apartment. On the fourth floor.'

'So that means…'

'I guess I have to find another place to live.'

'You're swapping Charles for Marilyn?'

'Hey, I'm not living with Charles,' she said. 'I'm not even

sleeping with him. He's just assumed all sorts of things I wasn't assuming. You know, I suspect my life's been leading up to this moment for years. I've spent my life pleasing my parents, pleasing my family, pleasing Charles. Then, this week, two shocks. A proposal of marriage. A near-death car crash. It's enough to give any girl an epiphany.'

'An epiphany,' he said faintly.

'Yep. Um... You know that painkiller?'

'Your foot really does hurt?'

'My foot really does hurt.'

Excellent. When in doubt, revert to priorities. Triage. Sore foot.

'Okay, painkillers,' he said, rising. 'You want me to carry you to the surgery?'

'Nope,' she said. 'No more of that, thank you very much. If I'm to be stuck here for Easter, I intend to be independent.'

'Fine,' he said, and had to suppress a jab of disappointment. Lifting Erin last night had been...an epiphany?

It wasn't anything of the sort, he told himself. It was simply because he was a male and she was a female and he'd been alone too damned long. Of course his body would react like...like it really wanted to get to know Erin better.

'No,' she said, and he blinked.

'Pardon?'

'Um...' She blushed suddenly and he stared down at her, fascinated.

'No, what?' he repeated, and she blushed some more.

'I didn't... I mean I was probably mistaken in what you were thinking. But if I'm not...' she said, fighting for recovery and becoming suddenly astringent. 'If I'm not then definitely no. Let's get back to basics. Do you want me?'

Did he want her? Yes and yes and yes.

'And enough of that, too,' she said astringently. 'You know very well what I meant. Do you want me as kid sitter, dog minder and medical associate over Easter?'

'Yes,' he said. And he wasn't saying a word more. This woman saw too much.

'Then painkillers followed by lunch,' she said. 'And then the boys and I might like to try making another batch of hot cross buns. This time with yeast. While you go and do your doctoring, wherever you do your doctoring.'

'I've told the locals I can't come out at Easter.'

'Then do your doctoring in your surgery,' she told him. 'Or paperwork or something. The boys and I will be in the kitchen. You're free to do as you like.'

'And if I want to be in the kitchen?'

'That's your choice,' she said, suddenly prim. 'But I'm offering you freedom to get your work done. It's my thanks for having me and Marilyn to stay. If you want to throw a gift horse in the mouth…'

'I believe that's look.'

'Sorry?'

'You don't throw gift horses,' he said, and suddenly she was pink again. He liked it, he decided. He really, really liked it.

'Whatever,' she said, sounding suddenly breathless. 'Same difference. All I'm saying, Dr Spencer, is that you're free to do what you want. Treat me as your cook and child companion for Easter and get on with your life.'

'Yes, ma'am,' he managed, and put a hand down to help her up.

She stared at it, appearing to consider. Then she slowly shook her head.

'Nope,' she said. 'While we're on platitudes…I don't intend to jump out of any frying pan into the fire.' Martin and Nathan were back at the door, looking hopeful. 'Boys, can you help me up?'

She turned her gaze away from his, she waited until the little boys gave her a hand apiece and she let them haul her to her feet.

While Dom looked on, feeling…jealous?

Ridiculous.

But jealous all the same.

CHAPTER FIVE

EVER since Tansy had told him she needed to take this time off, Dom had been dreading Easter. Normally the boys would be at school, and there'd be other kids' mothers he could call on to help. But Easter...nearly everyone was away or busy. He had Dulcie next door but Dulcie had her brother and sister-in-law visiting. She could come in for a real emergency but otherwise he was on his own.

Not only was he alone but the boys were bored. Their school friends were away. He didn't have time to spend with them and these kids were high maintenance.

But then came Erin. After he re-dressed her foot she settled into the kitchen. She downloaded hot cross bun recipes from the internet, discussed their merits with the boys, tried to figure why his might have failed—consensus was he'd warmed the dough in a too-hot oven—and then decreed she and the boys would try a recipe apiece. Luckily Tansy kept the pantry well stocked—when she saw it her face lit up.

'Ingredients. Yay!'

So they made three versions of bun, all of which worked. They decided—to Martin's delight—that Martin's was best, Erin's was second and Nathan's third—but they all ran rings round Dom's, no question.

He agreed, not even bothering to be offended. He and the boys were filled to the rim with bun. They squeezed a little soup in for dinner. They checked and rechecked Marilyn. The boys chattered to Erin like an old friend. She had them entranced and he didn't blame them.

He was close to entranced himself.

He should go out to Erin's wrecked car and fetch her belongings. He'd found her a toothbrush and comb—as an emergency foster-carer he always had necessities on hand—but she needed more. A change of clothes would be good. But the house was full of the smell of cooking and the sound of laughter and it seemed such…well, such a home that he wanted to stay.

It was an illusion, he thought, but he may as well enjoy it while it lasted.

The boys seemed mesmerised as well. When it was finally time for bed they left Erin with reluctance, but they knew she'd still be there tomorrow.

Tomorrow was looking great. It was so different from what he'd expected.

He'd seen six patients during the course of the day—none needing him to go out but each needing his full attention. Erin had turned the day around. She was fantastic, he thought, returning to the kitchen after tucking the boys in. A laughing, cheerful sprite…

He swung open the kitchen door and she looked so sad he stopped in his tracks.

'What's wrong?' he demanded involuntarily, and she caught herself and dredged up a smile.

'Nothing. Sorry. Just thinking. This is my thinking face.'

'It looks like your end-of-the-world face.'

'That's a bit dramatic.'

'Okay,' he conceded. 'Maybe it's a just-lost-your-fiancé face.'

'He's not my fiancé,' she snapped. 'He never was. He just assumed he was. He never told me, though. I've had boyfriends. He's had girlfriends. But of course he's always been around, and when I was offered this new job he decided I was getting too career oriented. It was time I knew where I stood. How's that for romantic?'

'Not very?' he said cautiously.

'Too right, not very. Is it dumb to want violins? Nightingales? Fireworks exploding? Isn't that what's supposed to happen?'

'I guess.'

'You mean it hasn't happened for you, either.'

'I think it's—'

'You tell me it only exists in the pages of a romance novel I swear I'll break down and sob,' she said darkly. 'I know this true love thing's out there somewhere. What about all those heroines out there dying of broken hearts? Or fading away of consumption.'

'Is that what you want to do?' He smiled at her mournful expression. 'If you do then maybe you need to cut down your intake of Easter buns.'

'And now you mock my romantic heart. It took only that.'

She was smiling now. But…behind the smile… There'd been real sadness when he'd walked into the room. He'd seen it.

He didn't need to get emotionally involved. This woman's life was not his business. He did not need to enquire any further.

Erin must be tired. He should tuck her into bed. No, whoops, dangerous. He should order her to bed. But his gut feeling was telling him the minute she was alone that face would return.

So, despite misgivings, he stayed. Erin was sitting by the stove, resting her feet on a footstool. He moved to stand beside her, back to the fire, a position he loved.

He couldn't think of a thing to say.

She was…beautiful.

Unaccountably, stupidly, he wanted to touch her. He wanted to run his fingers through her curls, tilt her face to his, kiss away her sadness…

Inappropriate, inappropriate, inappropriate.

He needed to get this on some sort of doctor/patient level, he decided. After all, that's what she was. She'd come to his house looking for medical help and he'd provided it.

So to kiss her now…

No.

'Your family and Charles's family are…close?' he ventured at last.

'Do you mind?'

'Just enquiring. There seems to be lots of undercurrents I'm not getting. I'm sniffing dysfunction. Dysfunctional families are my specialty. You want tea?'

'Sure,' she said, and watched him as he heated the teapot. 'Haven't you heard of teabags?'

'They don't work as well,' he said. 'For dysfunction.'

'My family's not dysfunctional.'

'You know, I'm a part-time dad,' he said. 'These kids are on loan while their families sort themselves out, but I still manage to get pretty close. If one of them sent word that he'd crashed his car, I might be tempted to find out for myself what was going on. It seems to me that your parents depended on Charles to report in. As far as I know, they haven't even phoned.'

'I'm almost thirty.'

'So when do you stop caring?'

'They do care.'

'Right.'

There was a long pause. He measured in scoops of tea with care. She eyed the pot with caution.

'They do,' she repeated at last. 'They care very much. It seems they're delighted I'm marrying Charles.'

'I thought you weren't.'

'I'm not. But according to Charles they think I am. Dom?'

'Yes.'

'Are you a complete paragon?'

'What do you mean?'

'Charles is very…controlled,' she said. 'He'd say drinking tea is really sensible right now.'

'You don't want tea?'

'I ought to want tea. It's very sensible of you to suggest tea.'

'But you'd rather…'

'Whisky,' she said promptly. 'Failing that, a glass of red. But, then…you probably disapprove.'

'Work of the devil,' he said, and loved the look on her face.

'Sorry,' she said meekly. 'Of course.'

'But if you could make do with some really excellent cognac…'

Her face changed again. She was totally transparent. He tried not to laugh but…she was making him laugh inside. It was an extraordinary sensation.

'You have cognac?' she demanded.

'For medicinal purposes only. Three times a day before meals or three glasses before bedtime. Whichever suits the patient.'

'Yes please,' she breathed. 'This patient needs medicine now.'

So they drank cognac. They also talked shop. Medicine was the easiest, safest thing to talk about.

They'd been to the same medical school, four years apart. How come he'd never noticed her? Mind, his head had been so far into books back then that he might not have noticed.

She was ambitious. She'd been one of the youngest graduates ever and she'd gone into emergency medicine.

'I love it,' she said. 'Pure adrenaline.'

'But you don't get to know your patients.'

'No. No emotional stuff that way.'

'You don't like emotional stuff?'

'I've had enough emotion to last me a lifetime.'

'You want to explain?' he asked, and she shook her head and stared into the depths of her cognac.

She fell silent. He didn't mind. He even liked it.

She was a restful woman. Warm and funny, but there were depths he could only guess at.

She'd used the comb he'd found her to good purpose. Her hair was lovely, tumbling around her shoulders in soft curls. More and more he wanted to reach out and touch… Reach out and kiss…

No. No and no and no.

'I lost my brother and sister,' she said bluntly, and her bald statement shook him out of his not so appropriate thoughts.

'How?'

'They were killed when I was four.' He had the impression she was trying to figure things out and he could listen or not. 'Sarah was seven and Connor was nine. Charles's father was driving. Charles was in the front seat. Charles was nine as well—he and Connor were friends. A truck ran a red light. Sarah and Connor were in the back seat and were killed instantly.'

'I'm so sorry,' he said, not knowing what else to say.

'I was too little to figure it out,' she said. 'I just remember people crying. Crying for years, really. And then, every family function since, Charles and his parents have been there.'

Ouch. A psychologist could have a field day with this one.

'So tonight…they'll all be distressed,' she whispered. 'They'll be sitting round not knowing what to think. But while you were putting the kids to bed I tried to ring, and Mum was so upset she wouldn't talk to me. Now Charles will be explaining I've had a shock and I'll come to my senses—he'll see to it. And my parents will listen to him. They'll leave me alone to figure things out. On about Easter Sunday Charles will appear again and be reasonable and have a very sensible plan as to what to do with Marilyn. What to do with me.'

Her voice wobbled.

He didn't get into this sort of emotion. But…as if it had a life of its own, his hand moved to rest gently on her hair.

She put her hand up and covered his.

It was okay. He could do this. It felt…right.

She needed this. He knew it. What he didn't understand so much was why he felt as if he needed it, too.

The urge for more…to take her in his arms, to kiss her, was still there, but it was supplanted. Comfort was okay. More than okay, actually. The warmth in this tangible link was so strong it left him feeling that something was being forged that was really important.

Something he wasn't sure existed.

'Dom,' she said at last, softly.

'Mmm?'

She pulled her hand away and maybe it was his imagination but he was sure there was reluctance. She had to move on.

They both did.

'I reckon Marilyn and her pups would be more comfortable in here by the stove,' she whispered. Then she tried again and she had her voice back. It made him wonder if the contact they'd had was disturbing her. She'd needed to get back to sensible. Practical. 'If we popped them in the corner they'd be out of the way. They can't stay in the hall all Easter. You want to cart them in?'

'I guess.'

So she sat by the stove and superintended while he made up a dog-bed. Gently he lifted each tiny pup across to the new bed, letting Marilyn see exactly what he was doing. As the last puppy was taken away from her, Marilyn heaved a doleful sigh, hauled herself to her feet and lumbered across to her new bed.

This felt okay, too, Dom thought. He was surrounded by domesticity and for once it didn't scare him.

He ought to go to bed. He'd been up since dawn and there was no guarantee he wouldn't be disturbed again during the night.

But he didn't want to leave the kitchen. He didn't want to leave Erin.

'So tell me about you,' she murmured.

And he thought, no, he should go.

'Not a lot to tell.'

'Yeah, there is. You finished med school four years before I did. Were your parents proud?'

'Ruby stood in the front row at my graduation and cried like her heart was breaking.'

'Ruby?'

'My foster-mother.'

'So your real mum and dad…'

'Disappeared years ago,' he said. 'I haven't heard from my mother since I was eight. My birth father was arrested for armed robbery six years ago. I read about it in the papers. But I only knew him by name.'

'Which explains why you take in foster-kids?'

'Maybe it does,' he said repressively.

'Did you always want to be a doctor?'

'Yeah.'

'Why?'

He shrugged. And then he thought, Why the hell not? Tell it like it is.

'We moved towns a lot when I was a kid,' he said. 'My mother was…not exactly stable.' He shrugged. 'She believed in love at first sight—which meant we followed loser after loser. Finally there was a night…' He hesitated, then decided there were still places he didn't want to go. 'Anyway, it was what the cops call a domestic. The police came, there were neighbours shouting, lots of stuff going on. And in the middle of it all, the doctor arrived. A nice, grey-haired old man who surveyed the mess, then came straight for me. I remember I was hiding under some hydrangeas in the corner of the garden. It was like he knew I had to be there. He came under the bushes, he told me I'd had enough, that he'd take care of my mum from now on, and then he put me in his car and took me to Ruby. I should have been taken in by Child Welfare. I should have been formally assessed. Instead, half an hour later I was by Ruby's fire-stove drinking mugs of hot chocolate while Ruby and the doctor talked about what colour socks he'd like her to knit him. And who was going to win the football that week.'

'He sounds wonderful,' Erin said in a voice that was suddenly none too steady.

'They both were,' he said. 'Doc Roberts and Ruby. Extraordinary people. I can't touch them for kindness. But I can take in the odd waif as payback.'

'How long have you taken in waifs?'

'Since I found Tansy,' he said. 'I was looking for a country practice. I wanted one where there was less work than there is here, but I came to the interview before I realised how remote it was. Tansy was on the panel that interviewed me. I mentioned I wanted space in my life to foster kids, and I wanted a big house. About two minutes later I had this place and a live-in housekeeper.'

'So she's bossy.'

'She's great.' He hesitated, feeling...exposed. Really exposed. 'But what about you?' he demanded, and his voice came out rougher than he'd intended. 'Why did you decide to be a doctor?'

'I don't think I ever had a choice. Two parents. One kid where there should have been three. Actually, four parents,' she said, 'for Charles's parents might as well have been my own. It was always assumed we'd do great things. Charles's parents knew he was going to be a doctor—though maybe that's unfair. Charles certainly wanted to be one. I got carried along for the ride.'

'But you like it?'

'I love it,' she said, and the dispirited tone gave way to sudden enthusiasm. 'I never thought I would, but I do. Mind, they're all desperately unhappy that I've chosen to work in emergency medicine rather than one of the status specialties. They think it's an aberration. Some day soon I'll settle to something more worthwhile.'

'An aberration,' he said, and turned and looked at Marilyn. 'You and your dog. Aberrations both.'

'What a thing to say.' Suddenly she smiled and, damn, there was that feeling in the depths of his gut again. It was the loveliest smile.

She was the loveliest woman.

But she was tired. The smile faltered almost as it appeared. She yawned—and Marilyn yawned in sympathy.

He smiled at the pair of them.

'Bed,' he said. 'Marilyn's in hers. I'll carry you to yours.'

'No need. I can manage.' She grabbed the crutches he'd found for her and struggled to her feet.

'No,' she said as he made a move to help her. 'Thank you, Dominic,' she said gently. 'You've been great.'

He didn't feel great. It nearly killed him to stay still and watch as she struggled out of the room. But somehow he did.

'Goodnight,' he said softly, and she turned and smiled.

'Goodnight, Dom,' she whispered. 'And thank you.'

She was gone. The kitchen felt bleak for her going.

Which was nonsense.

He made a desultory effort to clear dishes. He moved Marilyn's water bowl so she could reach it, and then as she stirred he thought okay maybe it was time, so he picked her up and carried her outside. She was moving herself now, but it filled a need to carry someone.

Erin for preference, but Marilyn was all that was on offer.

So he stood in the cool night air and waited until Marilyn completed her toileting. It was restful out under the stars.

He should feel peaceful.

Hell, he didn't. Erin was settling into bed right through that window. Erin…

Marilyn was sniffing the grass, licking up the dew, raising her head and smelling new smells. She looked battered and exhausted, yet profoundly grateful for this moment—for the ability to smell the night air before going back to her pups.

'Life's okay,' he said gently, and from the veranda came a response.

'It looks okay from this angle, too.'

He turned and Erin was watching him from under the porch lights.

She was lovely. Mind-blowingly lovely.

'You need to be in bed,' he said, and felt dumb.

'So do you.'

'So what's stopping us?' He lifted Marilyn again and carried her up the steps. The big dog looked up at him with an expression of something akin to devotion.

'Hey, don't look at me like that,' he told her. 'Doc Carmody here's the one who saved you.'

'And you saved us both.' Erin smiled at him and there it was again. Gut lurch.

Enough with the dog. Time for a little exercise rehabilitation. The door was open. He set Marilyn down, she waggled her butt and staggered toward the door.

Erin made a sharp move to clear a path but then it was her turn to stagger. She wobbled dangerously on her crutches and Dom made a dive. He caught her shoulders. Her crutches clattered to the floor—and he was left holding her.

'It's either one or t'other of us,' she said, sounding suddenly breathless. 'Me and Marilyn. Your walking wounded.'

'Or not walking. You want me to carry you to bed?'

'I don't think that's a good idea.'

'Why not?'

'I suspect you know why not,' she said, with a hint of asperity. 'You're too near, you're too male and you don't have a wife upstairs as chaperone.'

'Pity about that.'

'I'm sure you miss her madly,' she said, but she didn't pull away.

'I don't need anyone.' Where had that come from? The situation had been light. Suddenly it was intensely personal.

'I'm sure you don't,' she said softly. 'Whereas I…I need all sorts of people. So…so when does Tansy come back?'

'Her daughter had her baby last weekend. Maybe a couple of weeks.'

'I can't stay for a couple of weeks.'

'Of course you can't.'

'I should have gone with Charles.'

'You decided not to.'

'I did. I wanted to help you.' She sighed. 'Fat lot of help I am.'

'You did help. You are helping.' His hands stayed on her shoulders. She'd have to pull away if she wanted him to move and she wasn't pulling. She might even be leaning in.

He tugged her in a little bit further. Nice.

'Dom, I'm sorry I offloaded onto you,' she said softly against his chest. 'It wasn't fair. You've done so much for me, and here I am, keeping you from bed, asking for sympathy when you've got so much else on.'

'I don't have enough.'

'What, sympathy?'

'I'm not sure,' he said, looking down at her in the moonlight. 'I suspect sympathy is the least of it.'

'Me, too,' she said, unexpectedly—suddenly tentative. 'There's not a lot of sympathy happening from where I'm standing. I knew I had to apologise. Now I have. So…so maybe we could move on?'

A thought was occurring. An excellent thought. Maybe shared? Maybe crazy. Maybe not. Regardless, this was a thought worth airing.

'So if I were to kiss you…'

And, amazingly, she smiled. And nodded. A decisive little nod. Almost businesslike. 'It'd probably do us both the world of good. Like a tonic.'

'A tonic?' He was losing the thread.

'Something castor oil-ish. Something to give us both a decent purge. Reassure us we're okay.'

'You're asking me to kiss you or book you in for a colonoscopy?'

'Take your pick. I've imposed on your hospitality. It's up to you to name the price.' She grinned and raised her face. She jutted her chin in what he suspected was a gesture of defiance. To whom? To Charles? To her whole history? 'If it's not too much trouble.'

'It's definitely not too much trouble,' he said faintly—and then stopped speaking.

He had better things to do.

CHAPTER SIX

IT DIDN'T quite work.

He wasn't holding her tight enough. She slipped a little as their lips met; his mouth brushed hers, too briefly, and the kiss landed off centre.

She pulled back, just a little. 'Whoops.'

'Whoops?' It wasn't just his kiss that was off centre.

'I'm sorry,' she said, then eyed him sideways. 'I'm sorry. I'm strung up tight as a Stradivarius string.'

'Stradivarius?'

'Violin. You don't play?'

'No.'

'Thank God for that.'

'You don't like violins?'

'When other people play they're fine. But my parents dream of me playing when my music talent is more suitable for…I don't know…bongo drums.'

Funny. Interesting. Excellent dinner-party conversation.

Except they weren't at a dinner party. They were right here. Right now.

She might seem sure of herself, this woman, but talking violins when there was kissing to be done…that was nerves.

'Are we getting distracted?'

'I'm a bit nervous,' she conceded.

'Kissing's much easier than playing a violin,' he assured her. And before she could think of anything else to say, any other way to distract him—he tugged her tighter. He centred her so this time he couldn't miss—and he kissed her again.

Better didn't even begin to describe it. Better, better and better.

You didn't get to be thirty-five without learning how to kiss, Even though serious relationships weren't on his agenda, he'd had some very satisfactory frivolous ones—but nothing had prepared him for this. Not for the way she made him feel.

It was like he'd been zapped by an electric charge. If he could see himself in a mirror maybe his hair would be standing on end, he thought with the tiny amount of head room he had available for analysis. Which wasn't much, and what was available was getting less by the second.

He'd expected a kiss. But this was a...*kiss*.

From the moment his mouth met hers, nothing was as it had been. Nothing was as it should be.

What was that word? Discombobulated. He'd never used it. He needed it now.

For his thoughts were whirling, jumbled, out of kilter. His senses were centred solely on the fire inside, the fire this woman was creating. His brain felt short-circuited, circuits zapped and overlaid by sensations he'd never felt before.

This was a need he didn't know he had. She was melting into him and he was on fire. She was surrendering herself to him and it was the most exquisite gift...the most life-affirming generosity.

Her beauty stunned him. His hands caressed the small of her back and he thought he'd never known a woman as beautiful. Her breasts were melting against his chest and it was as if she was merging into him. Two bodies becoming one, fused by fire.

Her surrender was total. As his hands moved to her hips and tugged her closer he felt her rise to meet him, standing on tiptoe so her thighs were against his. He was responding with a fire he hadn't known he possessed.

She was the loveliest thing, the most beautiful woman, and amazingly she was opening herself to him, wanting him with a desperation that belied description.

But...

Desperation.

The word clanged into his head, unwanted, uncalled for, but suddenly there, loud and clear. He had an armful of the most desirable woman in the world but suddenly the instinctive knowledge of her despair was overwhelming.

Once thought, it couldn't be unthought.

She was letting herself sink into him to prove something to herself that had nothing to do with him.

How he knew it he couldn't say, but all of a sudden it was fact and the effect turned fire to ice.

How the hell he managed to stop, to pull away, he never knew, but somehow he did. He put her far enough so that he could look down into her eyes and see if the word he'd thought had any reality.

It did. She was gazing up at him, her eyes softly luminous, trying to smile, but there was confusion behind her smile. Her lip looked bruised, he thought. Had he kissed her so hard? She put her hands up to his head to tug him down to her again, but the sight of those bruised lips—of the confusion behind her smile—had him shaking his head.

'No.'

'N-no?' His pause had shaken her. He saw her bewilderment increase, and it was almost his undoing. She was here for the taking. She was a grown woman, a colleague who was surely old enough to know her own mind.

But still that word. Desperation.

'Erin, why are you doing this?'

'What...?'

'I'd take you to my bed in a heartbeat,' he said softly into her hair. Wanting desperately to increase the hold. 'But I know you're in trouble and I'm not sure you're kissing me for the right reasons.'

It was like tossing cold water over her. She pulled back a little, she gazed up at him for a long, bewildered moment and then slowly she tugged away. He released her with all the regret in the world.

'I don't know what you mean,' she managed, but he could see that she did.

'You're injured,' he said softly. 'You've come here as my patient...'

'No.'

'You came here last night because there was a sign on my front gate that said Doctor. Didn't you?'

'Of course I did,' she managed. 'But that doesn't mean—'

'I think it does mean. You're hurt. You came here for treatment and for refuge. For me to take advantage...'

'You're not taking advantage. Dom, you make me feel...'

'Yeah, well you make me feel, too,' he said ruefully. 'I do nothing but feel when I hold you. When I kiss you. But you're an emotional mess.'

'I am not!' It was said with such indignation that he almost laughed.

'Okay, you're not, so blame it on me. I don't want to feel like you make me feel. It's not that I'm not flattered...'

'Flattered,' she said, astounded.

'What man wouldn't be flattered?'

'So you're taking what just happened as...a compliment?' She gazed at him incredulously. 'You're not gay, I suppose?'

'No!'

'So my pride has to take it on the chin.'

'It's got nothing to do with pride.'

'Oh, yes it does,' she said bitterly. 'Here I was practically launching myself into your arms...'

'I believe I did some of the...launching.'

'Well, bully for you.' She sighed, a great gusty sigh that stunned him. She was like a chameleon, changing skins with mood. 'Okay, maybe it was a bad move.' She closed her eyes.

Moved on. 'So let's forget it ever happened, shall we? You'll still let me stay for Easter?'

'Of course I will.'

'Thank heaven for that. My noble host. Just when I want a hot one.'

'I'm sorry.'

She managed a smile at that. 'And now the man apologises… Where were you when I was planning my life? No,' she said, and put her hands up as if to ward him off. 'Don't answer. You were adopting kids, being noble, doing all sorts of stuff I can scarcely dream of.'

'You rescued Marilyn,' he reminded her. 'That has to count as noble.'

'So I did but it doesn't put me in your league. Nope. You're a wonderful man, Dr Spencer, and I admire you immensely. As one doctor to another. And you're right. We need to keep this professional. So…as patient to her treating doctor…or even as colleague to colleague…I need to go to bed. Goodnight.'

And without another word she turned and limped inside, down the hallway to her makeshift bedroom. Leaving Dom staring through the screen door after her.

Feeling like there was no way in the wide world he could forget the events of this night.

Feeling like his world had changed for ever.

How was a girl supposed to sleep after that? She couldn't. She lay and stared at the ceiling and thought of all the reasons why she should ring her parents and ask them to come and fetch her.

They would. They were upset with her now but they knew their duty. They'd be appalled by Marilyn but if she insisted, they'd take her. They'd drive her back to their own home on the outskirts of Melbourne.

They'd be dreadfully upset at having their Easter plans

spoiled, but maybe their Easter plans had been spoiled anyway. Maybe Charles had already hinted that Easter was to be the time of the Big Announcement.

And here she was, falling in love with another man.

Falling in love?

That was dumb. Crazy. Dom had pulled away because he'd sensed she'd felt desperate, and maybe he was right. Desperation, confusion, call it what you would.

Confusion. That's what it was. Because she'd never before felt like she felt when Dom smiled at her. When he'd kissed her it was like her world had blown apart.

It had scared her. Terrified her. She'd felt like she was teetering on the edge of a cliff and about to fall.

Into what? She didn't know.

Dom didn't want…permanence. He'd said that loud and clear.

Neither should she. She'd met the guy for the first time less than twenty-four hours ago. It was way, way too soon.

When, then?

When was the first proper time that she could open her eyes and say she'd fallen head over heels in love with Dominic?

How was a man expected to go calmly to sleep? Dom lay in his too-big bed and thought maybe he ought to trade it for a single. Hell, he had no use for a double, much less the king-sized opulence he lay in now.

He'd bought it thinking of Ruby, how early mornings had been a contest to see who could dive into Ruby's lovely squishy bed first. But he'd never got it right. He might do his damnedest as a foster-dad, but Ruby had something special.

Erin had something special.

She was as confused as he was. His family had been non-existent, a scattering of dysfunctional people vaguely connected by blood, but nothing else. Erin's extended family sounded much scarier.

He thought of the battered little boys in his care and he thought of Erin being raised with the ghosts of siblings. He wasn't sure which was worse.

What would be worse, though, he told himself, would be complicating his life by hitting on her. When he had no intention—no capacity—to take it further.

Why not? A spot of seduction, maybe even progressing to thinking about love?

Love.

For some reason that was what he was thinking—he, who'd never had such a thought before. But he was thinking it. Of loving Erin?

Was he nuts? What would he end up with? A woman torn by guilt, raised to be duty bound to two sets of parents and a man who regarded her as rightfully his.

Did Charles want her as much as he did?

It was a dumb question. The whole situation was impossible.

He'd made a vow, a long time ago, when he'd been used as a bitter connection, a rope in domestic tugs of war where neither his mother nor his string of stepdads had worried that he might snap. Domestic harmony was for others—he wasn't even going to try.

He'd had the odd relationship—who hadn't? Until now he'd never wanted to push it an inch further than a casual affair.

So why was Erin different?

Because she was damaged, he told himself fiercely. He saw in her the same need he saw in his boys, maybe even in himself, but need was no basis for a relationship.

She was here as his guest, using him for refuge. Therefore he had to apply the same rules he applied to his boys. All care but no ties, so when they left there was no heartbreak on either side.

And as for the love word… When he'd known her for such a short time… That was being no better than his mother. Love at first sight was a crazy ideal, leading to heartbreak all round.

Right. He had that clear.

Maybe tomorrow he could drive her to her parents' place himself. Or not.

Probably not.

She'd offered to help. He needed help. There was a very sensible reason for him to accept her offer.

It was sensible for her to stay.

Yeah, right.

She slept badly, dozing and waking, dozing and waking. Once she heard Dom pad downstairs and let Marilyn out into the garden.

He was a very nice man, she told herself dreamily in her half-sleep. She listened to him leading Marilyn back to her pups, then speak softly. She couldn't hear, but she was willing to bet there wasn't any mention of dog pounds.

If she was seriously interested...

Dom with his needy kids... Marilyn and her needy pups...

Dom.

She was seriously interested. Dumb or not.

'Maybe I need to go to the Antarctic for a year,' she muttered. 'I can hone my skills with frostbite and hypothermia, and everyone can need me solely because I wield a great roll of sticky plaster.'

But...how could she go the Antarctic when there was the faintest possibility of a repeat of that kiss?

Dumb or not, she was staying right where she was. For as long as Dom let her.

Easter Saturday.

Dom was coolly pleasant at breakfast. If he could be coolly pleasant, she could too, she decided. He didn't say anything about leaving, and if he didn't, neither would she.

Even though he'd told the locals he wasn't doing calls, he was still the only doctor in the district. Patients arrived with the minor trauma of a country community. The phone never stopped. She ended up fielding calls—and enjoying it.

'You've had a sore knee for months? Dr Spencer will be happy to see you, but not until Tuesday. He's busy right now.'

Actually, the doctor was examining puppies when that call came. Dom's vet-friend, Fiona, had found an excuse to drive over and check for herself that her instructions had been carried out. Dom and the elderly vet were checking each individual pup. Erin had been the one closest to the phone and Dom seemed okay— even grateful—that she answer it. She glanced through to the kitchen as she replaced the receiver. Dom looked a query—doctor examining patients while stretched out on the kitchen floor in front of woodstove. He smiled at her. Her heart did a silly backward somersault—and she was suddenly even more determined to stay.

Any more determined they'd soon have to prise her out of here with a chisel, she thought. Superglue had nothing on how she was starting to feel.

After Fiona left, at Dom's suggestion they took a family drive. No, make that a communal drive, she corrected herself. This was not a family—Mum and Dad in the front and kids in the back. Regardless, they headed out to her crashed car. Yesterday her feet had been too sore, she had been too shocked and Marilyn had needed supervision, but she really wanted her clothes.

In the daylight the crash scene looked appalling. She'd been dead lucky. She and the boys watched as Dom climbed down the river bank and retrieved her overnight bag from the trunk—and her cellphone and her shoe.

'A good scrub and it'll be good as new,' he said, handing over a blood-stained, mud-soaked trainer.

'Yum,' she said, taking the shoe gingerly. He grinned again and there it was. Slam. Backward somersault—with pike this time.

They returned to the house. Dom saw a couple more patients. She tried not to think about that grin.

She answered the phone and she baked.

There was something really therapeutic about baking on a firestove. She couldn't figure what it was, but her foot felt better every minute she spent there.

The little boys loved it, too. She was getting comfort as well as giving it, she thought, watching them wrap themselves round meatloaf and apple pie for lunch. Dom asked for a second helping of pie, he smiled again…and wham.

This had to stop. It was making her dizzy. She was out of her depth, diving too hard, too fast and not knowing where she was going.

She met Dom's gaze and his smile faded.

He's just as confused as I am, she realised, and the idea was…unsettling.

Dom was clearly unsettled. He took himself back to his surgery to catch up on paperwork.

He had too much work to do. Far too much for one doctor.

An idea was seeding in the back of her brain. She refused to give it countenance. It was too soon. Way too soon.

Concentrate on the kids, she told herself. Concentrate on anything but the way Dom's smile made her feel. And this tiny germ of an idea…ridiculous.

Martin was quiet, passive. They played Scrabble and did a jigsaw puzzle and Martin grew quieter. Nathan helped her cook corn fritters for dinner, but Martin watched, silent. Then they settled down with books in front of the living-room fire.

Finally Dom joined them. He had a couple of kids' books to read out loud. Nathan enjoyed them but Martin was getting quieter.

She was flicking through a magazine—this month's *Family Doctor*. Riveting stuff. She could sort of read while she sort of watched.

Martin looked strained. Why? She watched Dom, who was clearly worrying about him. At eight he lifted Martin from where he'd been drooping by the fire. He took Nathan's hand and bade her goodnight.

'You're coming back down?' she asked, startled, and he shook his head.

'I have a lot of medical journals to catch up on.'

'So catch up on them here.'

'It's distracting here,' he said gently. 'I can't afford to be distracted.'

Ouch.

'But we've really appreciated your help today,' Dom said, still in that gentle, reasonable voice that made her want to hit him. 'Haven't we, boys?'

'Yes,' Nathan said, definite, but Martin burrowed his face into Dom's shoulder and didn't say anything.

'Erin cooks great meals, doesn't she?' Dom said, pressuring Martin to respond.

There was a faint sniff, miserable. 'She's like my mum.'

Oh, heck. Whatever was going on in this little boy's background, one thing stood out. He missed his mother with all his heart. Those four words had been a cry like from a little boy lost.

'I know you do,' Dom said softly, and he looked at Erin over Martin's head and gave his own head an imperceptible shake. Meaning there's nothing she could do to help.

There wasn't.

She watched them go upstairs and she ached. She wanted to help so much it hurt.

She'd been here for a day. What right did she have to mess with these people's lives?

What right did she have to ache to be a part of theirs?

She remade her settee. She went out and said goodnight to Marilyn. She climbed into bed and tried to sleep.

It was too early. There was too much in her head. Like how to get close to this little family? Like who was Tansy—where did she fit? Like how much Dom needed her. Like how one guy could cope with such a medical practice and still have time for these kids?

Over and over the image of Dom played in her head—the

sight of him comforting Martin, the memory of him smiling at her that morning when he'd been examining the puppies, the way he was just...Dom.

She sat up and read about six of the kids' books, trying to get herself tired. She lay down again and watched the flames.

Dom. Dom, Dom, Dom.

She was going nuts. She put her head under her pillow and groaned.

Finally she slept. But when she slept she dreamed of Dom.

She woke up to fire.

CHAPTER SEVEN

MAYBE the fireplace was smoking. It was her first thought, but it was fleeting. The fire in the hearth was almost dead—a soft glow of coals and nothing more. But the smell of smoke had intruded on her half-sleep and Marilyn was barking.

She stumbled out of bed, worried, and the fire alarm started as she reached the door. She flung open the door into the hall, the faint smell of smoke became a thick wall of fog and the scream of the smoke alarm became almost deafening.

From the kitchen Marilyn let out a yowl of distress but the smoke wasn't coming from the kitchen, either. It was billowing down from the top of the stairs. The security lights on the stairs and in the entrance were showing a faint sheen of smoke around her feet, but at head height the smoke was already so thick she could scarcely see.

'Dom,' she screamed—entirely without need when the fire alarm was doing her screaming for her. She hit the stairs, two at a time, forgetting about her injured feet, forgetting everything except that Dom and the boys were somewhere in the midst of the source of the fire.

'Dom…'

The cry was from one of the kids, a terrified scream, high and filled with horror. She was at the landing now, her hand on the balustrade, feeling her way rather than seeing.

And then the smoke swirled back and Dom was there. An armload of child was thrust at her. Nathan. She clung and steadied and Dom was already invisible.

'Ring emergency services,' he snapped from the gloom. 'Get Nathan outside, and the dog. I need to find Martin.'

He was gone.

She staggered down the stairs again, carrying Nathan. He had his arms round her neck, holding on as if his life depended on it, sobbing with fear. As she hit the flat surface of hall she staggered a little with the weight of him, and he clung tighter still.

She groped for the phone—she had a clear idea where it was now, which was just as well as the smoke was so thick she'd never have found it by sight.

'Fire,' she snapped into the phone without waiting to hear the operator ask leading questions. She gave ten seconds of curt directions. 'Repeat it,' she ordered, with the same efficiency she used with interns when she had to make sure they understood in an emergency.

Marilyn was whining, agitated, in the kitchen. Erin shoved open the door; the dog pushed her nose against her leg and then headed back to her pups.

'We need to get us safe,' she said to Nathan, trying to figure what to do next. Somewhere upstairs were Dom and Martin, but by the way Nathan was clinging and sobbing she knew he wouldn't let her go. 'I'll take you onto the veranda.'

'No,' Nathan whimpered, but there was no time for sympathy. She should take Nathan outside, leave him, then go to help Dom, but she knew he'd come back in after her.

And Marilyn was clearly a dog in panic.

Okay. She had to let Dom take care of Martin as best he could until she had Nathan safe. The only way to get Nathan safe was to anchor him.

Anchor him to Marilyn. Anchor Marilyn with the puppies.

She bent over the pups, setting Nathan firmly on the floor

beside her. 'Nathan, hold my shirt and don't let go,' she snapped before he could clutch her round the neck again. 'Don't move away from me. I'm picking up the puppies.'

She tugged Marilyn away from the pups, and before Marilyn could react she gathered pups—bed included—against her. She now had an armload of blanket and pups, a little boy clutching her shirt and Marilyn making a Herculean effort to jump up and get to her babies.

And there was smoke. She was struggling to breathe without gagging. She wanted to hold her shirt over her mouth but she had no hands left.

'Let's go,' she muttered, and headed out the door. In seconds she was out on the front veranda, with Nathan towed behind her and Marilyn leaping anxiously about her feet.

The relief to find herself outside was almost overwhelming. She kept going, over the grass, well away from the front door. Near the gate she allowed herself to pause.

'Dom, Dom, Dom,' she found herself saying, swinging round to face the house and hoping against hope he was following.

The lights in the upstairs windows flickered and went out. The power was gone.

At least she couldn't see flames. There was an almost full moon in a cloudless sky and the house was a great, unlit shape.

No flames.

'You need to stay here,' she told Nathan, and he whimpered and clung, but she put him away from her, mustering strength before she started to speak. If she sounded scared there was no use expecting courage from him.

She laid the puppies on the ground by the gate. Marilyn whined her distress and started doing a maternal tongue count.

'I have to help Dom bring Martin out,' she said to Nathan, keeping her voice flat, inflexionless, like this was a completely normal scenario. 'But Marilyn has to stay here. Can you put your hand in her collar and not let her move until I get back?' She tucked his hand under the dog's frayed collar. 'Promise you won't let her go? She might still think there's a puppy inside and run in after me. It's too smoky inside to be safe.'

'You'll come back?'

'Of course I'll come back.' She gave him a swift, hard hug. 'With Dom and Martin. But you're in charge of Marilyn and puppies. Can I trust you?'

'Y-yes.'

'You're great, Nathe,' she said.

'Erin…'

'Mmm.'

'Will you save the Easter eggs, too?'

The smoke had increased so much it was terrifying. It was a thick, flat wall, oozing out the door, stinking, grit-filled and dreadful.

She got three feet inside the front door and backed out. She'd make it maybe ten feet without a plan. If that.

Plan. Right. Like wait until the fire brigade arrive and men in uniform take over?

Not an option.

She leant on the wall of the front veranda and took three, four, lungfuls of cleanish air and then decided what were lungs if not to be used.

'Dom!' she screamed at the top of her voice. *'Dom!'*

Nothing. He'd hardly be able to scream back if he was in the pall of smoke inside.

So think. Layout of house. She hadn't been upstairs apart from that one brief foray to get Nathan. She was going to have to feel her way.

She hauled back and checked the upstairs windows again. No orange glow. Lots of smoke. She could contend with that.

The downstairs bathroom was right next to the front door. Head there first and wet towels.

No. Wool would be better. Back into the sitting room. Blankets.

She was back beside her makeshift bed almost before she thought it, grabbing blankets, feeling her way back out into the bathroom, tossing the blankets into the shower, turning on the tap, then getting herself back outside for another couple of lungfuls of air while the blankets soaked.

'Stay, Nathan,' she breathed, but there was no time to check he was following directions. She was inside again, hauling sodden blankets out from the shower, draping them over her head, then groping her way along the hall toward the stairs.

Underneath the dripping blankets she could at least breathe, and she managed to call. 'Dom. Dominic!'

'Erin!'

The call, ending on a choked cough, had her feeling her way up the stairs again, clinging to the balustrade, blind under her canopy of wet wool.

'Dom...'

He was on the top step. Crouching as she was. She almost fell as her feet came into contact with his solid presence. A hand came out and caught her ankle.

She was crouched low but now she sank even further, her hands seeking contact.

Her hands met his. Fingers clasping momentarily in the gloom. Registered the wetness.

'Great forethought, Dr Carmody,' he managed, the words coming out as a hoarse, choking gasp.

'I have two.' She tugged one of the sodden blankets from her shoulders.

He grabbed it. Hauled it over himself. 'I can't find him,' he breathed. 'There's only Tansy's room left. Stay here.'

'I'm coming.'

'Don't be stupid. But stay here unless it gets so bad you can't breathe at all. I might need help carrying...'

He didn't waste further breath. He was gone.

Leaving her to wait. And wait.

Maybe it was only seconds but it was the longest wait of her life. Crouched at the head of the stairs. Not knowing the layout of the house. Knowing if she moved, Dom might well end up hunting for her.

Hearing the first crackle of flames.

Terror...

And then Dom was there. Magically. Hauling her wet blanket up, pushing a limp body into her arms. Martin.

'I...I can't...' Dom stuttered. 'I need...a minute. Go. Get him out.' He was out from under her blanket, leaving Martin behind, and she heard him beside her, choking, lungs desperate for air.

He'd come from the seat of the fire, she thought. If she was struggling to breathe, the fact that Dom had managed to haul the child to her was nothing short of miraculous.

They couldn't relax yet. Martin was limply unconscious. She hauled him close under her blanket. Smoke was pouring through.

'Go,' Dom muttered.

'You follow,' she gasped, and as he didn't move she struck out with her foot, kicking so hard she heard him gasp in pain. 'You follow or I'm not moving. Don't you dare give in. Move.'

She could do no more. She was sliding down the stairs, clasping Martin to her, bumping on her backside, afraid to stand, not knowing what was in front or what was behind, not knowing if Dom was able to follow but knowing only she had to get outside before she lost consciousness. How many stairs? She sagged and something hit her in the small of the back.

Dom was behind her. 'I can take him now,' he muttered. 'I'm okay.'

'Pigs might fly,' she managed, and focused on the next step.

The knowledge that Dom was right behind her was enough to get her down the last three stairs into the hall. She fell sideways on the last stair, rolled, tugging Martin with her, and kept going, hauling him out through the front door and onto the veranda.

She couldn't stop. She couldn't wait for Dom. Even here it wasn't safe. The smoke was billowing outward, a tunnel of acrid poison. She was blind, still unable to remove her blanket. She shoved herself sideways, away from the door, tugging the dead weight of the child along with her.

One last tug and she was over the side of the veranda, dropping the eighteen inches or so into the flower bed below, out of the path of the smoke, out into clean, clean air...

Martin fell with her. Still. Ominously limp.

'Oh, Martin...' She was sobbing with fear and desperation. She tugged him free of the bushes so she could assess clearly what was happening.

She searched for a pulse. It was there...

And suddenly it wasn't.

One part of her was blinded by panic, horror struck, terrified for Dom as well as for Martin. The rest of her was moving into medical mode. Checking airway, shifting the little boy into a position where she could work.

'You're going to live,' she muttered fiercely. 'Dom didn't save you for nothing.' She pinched his nose, put her mouth over his and breathed until his chest rose.

One breath. Fifteen pumps on his chest. Hard, fierce, determined.

Breathe, damn you, breathe, but she didn't have the strength to say it. She bent again and breathed hard, filling those small lungs, then shifted to thump again...

'I'll do it.'

And miraculously Dom was there, edging her aside so he could work on Martin's chest. 'I'll do CPR,' he croaked. 'You keep breathing.'

It was like a gift from heaven. Dom was safe. Dom was with her.

One life safe. One to go. Please.

They had much more chance of succeeding with two of them. She'd have more clear air in her lungs than Dom did, she acknowledged, although surely she must be stronger than he was right now. How could he have the strength to perform CPR?

'If you're not risking cracking ribs, you're not thumping hard enough.' It had been one of her first lectures.

But Dom was thumping hard enough, strongly and steadily, as if he had all the energy he needed and then some.

Breathe. Thump, thump, thump.

There was a desperate whimper from behind her. Nathan. It was too dark, too smoky, to see, but she could hear his terror.

'Nathe,' she managed between breaths. 'Can you look down the road to see if the fire brigade is coming? Then stay with Marilyn to stop her getting frightened. We're okay.'

There was a grunt of approval from Dom but there was room for nothing else.

Breathe. Thump, thump, thump. Breathe. Thump, thump…

How was he doing it? The man had almost died himself. For him to give Martin to her at the head of the stairs…she had no doubt he'd been feeling close to the edge himself.

People did extraordinary things under pressure. Stories came back to her…mothers lifting cars off their children. Running when running was otherwise impossible. Life or death—the threat gave superhuman abilities.

The need to perform a miracle…that was what they needed. A miracle. She breathed again, cupping the little boy's chin, tilting it, pushing the breath down, hoping, hoping…

And then…a tiny gasp. A jerk.

A cough. His eyes fluttered open.

'Martin,' Dom said in a voice she didn't recognise.

'Dom,' the little boy faltered, and then he was thickly, splendidly ill.

And suddenly it was over. The threat was past. There was nothing more for her to do. Dom was supporting his foster-son, tugging him in against him, cradling him so he couldn't choke, soothing, holding, holding.

'Nathe,' she called into the dark, and Nathan came flying back to her.

'Hey,' she said, and tugged the little boy into her own arms. 'These two are going to be okay. We've rescued each other.'

And then she hugged him so hard she thought she might break one of his ribs and Dom was reaching out to touch her. She hauled herself closer, tugging Nathan close with her and they sat in a huddle of mess and soot and smoke and she thought she'd never felt happier. And when Marilyn appeared through the mists of smoke, signifying her presence by a slurp to the face, she grabbed her, too, and the dog was enveloped in their sandwich squeeze as well.

'Hey,' Dom managed in a voice that was full of smoke and fear and the remnants of toxins. 'We're all okay. Thanks to our wonderful Erin.'

'Thanks to all of us,' she replied, kissing Nathan's hair. What she really felt like doing right now was kissing Dom but it was hardly appropriate. So she just sat within the circle of eight arms and Marilyn's tongue and felt fabulous, and then the sirens started in the distance and the cavalry was here.

CHAPTER EIGHT

FIRST came a fire engine, screaming though the dark, screeching to a halt at the front gate, sending floodlights over the scene and disgorging maybe fifteen men and women, all in various states of undress. They were donning uniforms as they climbed from the vehicle, Erin saw from the safety of her under-veranda sanctuary. They'd be local volunteers, roused out of their beds, expecting anything.

'We're over here,' she tried to call, but her voice wasn't working properly, and then she saw them heading toward the gate and Marilyn's puppies were right in the way.

'Go stop them,' Dom said, and she cast him a look of desperation. Because that was how she felt. Desperate. Her voice didn't work. She wasn't sure her legs would work.

'The boys are safe here with me,' Dom said. 'Save the puppies.'

How did he know where the puppies were?

But then she looked out through the smoky haze and Marilyn was making a beeline for the gate and she thought it wouldn't take much of Dom's intelligence to figure out that's where the puppies were.

'Go,' he said, and he reached out and touched her face in a fleeting gesture that could mean anything at all but it meant everything. It gave her the strength to pull herself up and stagger across the garden after Marilyn.

'Watch your feet,' she managed to scream, and the front fire-fighter stopped dead, long enough for her to reach the puppies and gather them up again into her arms. Poor Marilyn. This was not an ideal maternity hospital, she thought grimly, but at least they were alive.

And help was at hand. The lead firefighter was in front of her, his hands on her shoulders, his face grim and his voice sharply authoritative.

'Is anyone inside?'

'We're all out,' she managed. She tried to turn, and he relaxed his grasp, but only a little. And indeed if he'd released her completely she might have toppled over. 'They're by the veranda.'

'Doc?'

'And the two boys. In the garden by the steps. The fire's upstairs.'

'Put her behind the truck,' the guy growled to someone behind him and she was placed firmly into the hold of someone else. Someone propelling her out of the way.

'I need to go back to Dom.'

'We'll bring Dom to you,' the man said.

And in minutes they did. She was sitting where she'd been led, on the far side of the fire truck, feeling reaction set in, feeling sick, holding an armload of puppies and with Marilyn draped over her legs.

Dom was carrying Martin, and a firefighter was carrying Nathan.

Martin was fully conscious now. His eyes were huge, full of fear. Only Nathan was no longer fearful. With terror past, this was a small boy's dream. Firefighters and engines and fire.

For Martin it looked to be the stuff of nightmares.

'We've rung an ambulance,' the firefighter told Dom, but Dom shook his head and lowered himself to sit beside Erin, still holding Martin hard against him.

'We won't need an ambulance,' he said, firm and sure. 'Martin's okay now. He passed out through smoke inhalation but he's looking good. If you can grab my emergency bag from the back of my car I'll give him some oxygen. You know I'm a doctor, Graham. I can take care of him.'

'But…' Erin paused. Martin had come close to dying from smoke inhalation. If she'd had him in her emergency department she'd be wanting oxygen, X-rays, intensive care type observation for the night.

Dom would know the score as well as she did. He'd know there was a possibility they'd cracked ribs. Why…?

And then she looked at Martin, who was shivering against Dom, deathly pale, terrified. Dom was weighing relative risks, she realised. Keep him here and run the risk of complications—or send him to hospital and maybe cause even more trauma. If his mother had been harming him to draw attention to herself… This child must have had enough of hospitals for life.

Okay. She'd go with Dom on this one.

'How much oxygen do you have here?' she asked, and he flashed her a look that said he knew what she was thinking, but he knew what he was doing.

'Enough to send the local football team scuba diving for a week or so.'

She refused to smile. She needed to focus. 'Can you do a chest X-ray here?'

'Yes.'

'Okay, then,' she conceded. 'I concur.'

The tension in Dom's face eased a little. 'Great.'

Above them, the firefighter was frowning. 'If you're sure…'

'I'm sure,' Dom said. 'Just go save my house.'

'I'm a doctor, too,' Erin told him. 'I'll take care of them.'

The man cast her a look that said frankly he didn't believe her. Maybe she wouldn't either, she thought drily. She was wearing pink pyjamas—silk. She was covered in soot and she was wrapped in a huge grey army blanket. Doctor? Sure.

'It really is okay,' Dom said. 'Erin helped me with Jamie

Sutherland yesterday. You've probably heard. She's more than competent. Amazingly I seem to have a colleague.'

'Well, about bloody time,' the man said, and gave Erin a grin. 'Welcome to Bombadeen, Doc. You sure are welcome.' He gave her a salute, part gentle mockery but there was thanks and admiration in there as well—and disappeared back to the action. Another firefighter brought Dom's equipment, and they were left alone.

Which was…weird.

Sitting in a huddle on the far side of the biggest of the fire engines, it was as if they were in a cocoon of isolation, cut off from the drama being played out on the other side of the truck. Men were shouting, orders were being thrown, flashlights were augmenting the floodlights—it seemed the press had arrived. There was organised chaos as the firefighters went about their business. Floodlights were playing over the house, but here they were in shadow.

They were in a tight huddle. Dom had Martin hugged tight against him. Erin had checked Martin's lungs. She'd put on an oxygen mask on him, but Martin was recovering by the minute. Thank God.

Dom was sitting with his back against the truck's rear tyre, and involuntarily Erin shifted closer—close enough so she could feel the comfort of his big body against hers. She was holding Nathan but the feel of one little boy wasn't enough contact. She needed as much reassurance as she could get.

She needed to feel that she wasn't alone, that the terror of the fire was over.

Marilyn was settling down amidst her puppies, nuzzling each, doing her eternal check, and the dog's rump was firmly settled against her leg. Marilyn, too, it seemed, needed comfort.

'Hey, more blankets,' someone called from the shadows, and produced a pile of thick wool to spread over all of them. Dry, soft wool. Lovely.

Amazingly Nathan was back to being himself. He wriggled out of their grasp and ventured to the end of the fire truck, taking a blanket with him. Erin watched his small face transform from fear and shock to wonder. Firefighters. Hoses, pumps, water…

He was a small boy again, and this was an adventure.

Not for her, yet. Not for Martin and not for Dom. She sniffed, feeling a bit desperate, and Dom's arm came round her shoulders.

'It's okay,' he said softly. 'We're safe. Thanks to you.'

'I didn't…'

'You know, smoke makes you want to be sick,' Dom said thoughtfully, his hand putting pressure on her shoulders in a silent warning that he was no longer talking to her—that he had a plan. 'It's horrid. Being sick is horrid. Being burned is horrid.'

She sensed, rather than saw, Martin tense in Dom's arms. Nathan was out of earshot but there was no way Martin was ready to call this an adventure.

'I'm guessing you made a little fire, Martin,' Dom said softly, and in the eerie, deflected light from the floodlights she saw the little boy's eyes flare.

'I didn't…'

'I think you did,' Dom said, and amazingly his tone was conversational. Matter-of-fact. 'In the blanket box in Tansy's room.'

'It was only a little fire,' Martin whispered. 'I thought it would hurt me just a little bit. But then I got scared and hid in the cupboard.'

'And that was really, really sensible,' Dom said, still matter-of-factly. 'Because who wants to be hurt? If you'd hurt yourself you would have had to go to hospital and Nathan and I would miss you.'

'You'd come and sit by me. You'd give me stuff.'

'We give you more stuff when you're here,' he said. 'Lots more stuff. Hospital's lonely.'

'My mum was in hospital.'

There were depths here she hadn't dreamed of. Erin found she was forgetting to breathe. Oh, Martin…

Oh, Dom.

'I'm thinking Erin reminded you of your mum,' Dom said softly. 'Your mum's very sick. That's bad, but what's worse is that sometimes she made you sick or hurt too, so she could go to hospital with you. That was part of her sickness. But now you live with people who aren't sick. People who try really hard to stay well. Because it's more fun. Do you like living with us?'

'Yes.' Then, almost defiantly, 'Yes! And I don't like being sick. I didn't want to be burned. I was scared.'

'No one wants to be sick. If you're sick you can't run, swim, jump on your pogo stick, make the best Easter buns in the world. From now on you have to stay well so you can do all those things.'

Dom was stroking Martin's hair, softly, softly. His hands were stained black, his face was grimed, he'd come close to death himself, but it seemed now that he had all the time in the world. This man was the gentlest man she'd ever met, Erin thought.

She'd thought she'd met the most caring of doctors.

She was wrong.

'Dom went all through the house to find you, Martin,' Erin whispered, guessing there'd been healing tonight but instinctively guessing there was room—even a need—for lightness now. For both Dom and for Martin. 'Dom wore a big, wet blanket and he crawled through the house looking for you. He looked like a big, wet bear.'

'And Erin looked like a littler bear,' Dom said, seeing where she was going and going with her. 'She crawled, too. Mummy and Daddy Bear looking for Baby Bear in the cupboard.'

And suddenly, amazingly, Martin managed a smile. A bit watery. A bit pale, but a smile for all that.

'I'm not a baby bear. I'm not fuzzy enough.'

Dom chuckled.

It was an amazing sound.

Erin blinked and suddenly her eyes widened and she looked at him—she really looked at him—and the thought came to her with such blinding clarity it almost hurt.

This guy's awesome.

And…

I could really, really love this guy.

And…

Stupid or not, I think I already do.

Dom was hugging Martin and smiling, but suddenly his gaze shifted and he was looking at her. Their gazes locked and she knew she ought to look away but she didn't.

Big, gentle, kind, clever, he was so damned sexy that if the kids weren't here she could have had him on the spot.

It must be the shock, she thought, stunned. To be thinking of jumping him, right here, right now…it was totally inappropriate.

But, oh, if she could…

He was looking a question. She tried to pull herself together—and failed.

'I…I…' She couldn't think of what to say next.

'Are you okay?'

'No,' she managed. 'I'm a bit shocked. I'm a bit full of smoke. If…if you don't mind I need to go see if the house is still standing. It… Maybe it's important.'

'We're all fine,' Dom said. He couldn't move. He had his arms full of Martin but Erin was so choked up, the need to leave was imperative. She went to rise but Dom's hand came out and gripped her wrist, holding her down.

'You really are okay?' he demanded, sounding worried.

'I really am okay,' she managed. 'I'm just a bit…a bit… Well, we're fine. But if you don't mind, I left my shoes in the house and I need to see if the firemen have saved them.'

'Your shoes,' Dom said blankly.

'And my Easter egg,' Nathan said from behind them.

'And my pogo stick,' Martin whispered.

'Of course,' Erin said. 'See? I need to save shoes and egg and pogo stick.'

'But—'

'I need to go, Dom,' she said, more urgently this time, but then as his hold on her wrist tightened she couldn't help herself.

She turned to face him, head on. His face was right there. His eyes were on a level with hers. His mouth

Yeah, okay, his mouth. Inappropriate, inappropriate, inappropriate.

What the hell. He was tugging her closer.

She let herself be tugged.

And kissed.

What had she expected?

A feather kiss? A kiss of reassurance, friendship? It stood not a snowball's chance in a bushfire of being anything so tame. His kiss—his demanding hold—his touch—were an affirmation of the blast of emotion that had just hit her.

His kiss was…hers.

That's what it felt like. Here was an unlocked link, an open part of her that had been left free, waiting for the right connection. It was a connection of heat, of want, of need, of everything she'd been waiting for all her life. Here it was, in this one kiss.

In this one man.

Everything faded. Everything.

To an observer maybe the kiss was light. She couldn't melt against him—Martin was already there. She was somehow kissing him—being kissed—over the top of Martin's head. But Dom's kiss was as demanding as hers, taking comfort, taking heat, taking whatever she had to give.

Dom. Her hero.

Her man.

In the last couple of days, her world had been blasted apart. Or maybe her world had been blasted apart twenty or more years ago with the death of her brother and sister, and maybe it had taken until now to come out from under the rubble. Since her siblings' deaths she'd been drifting, trying to make sense of everything, but nothing quite had. She'd been trying to make herself three people.

But she couldn't be what she was supposed to be. Her tumble down the cliff had shown her just how stupid that ambition was. She'd nearly died. And now again tonight… This was the only life she had. This was her life. Hers.

And now it felt like she was giving that life away—but gaining so much in return. Dom. A life for a life. It felt right, it felt wonderful, and it felt like the other half of her whole had slipped magically into place.

The kiss extended far past the point where a casual kiss would have stopped. For she couldn't break the link. Dom was leaning against the fire truck, his arms full of Martin, his legs draped with dog, but he was kissing her just as much as she was kissing him. Their mouths were fused in a searing blast of heat that left the rest of her weak and useless. Every fibre of her being was focused on that kiss.

Somewhere behind them a window broke. The smash of broken glass hauled them out of their thrall. If it hadn't, maybe they'd still be kissing. For both of them this night had meant terror, and in this kiss both of them had found release.

But it was more than that.

As Erin pulled back she knew it was far, far more than that. But Dom was looking confused, and the boys were looking at her in confusion as well.

'Kiss us, too,' Nathan whispered, and she gave a shaky laugh and did just that.

'Of course. 'Cos we're great.' She kissed Nathan on the tip of his nose; she kissed the subdued Martin on the top of his head; and then, for good measure, she kissed Marilyn's weird, squashed nose as well. 'We're all fantastic. Now, if you don't mind, I really need to go find a pogo stick and some eggs.'

CHAPTER NINE

AMAZINGLY the fire had been contained to one room.

'It's all smoke,' the firefighters told her. 'The seat of the fire is a store chest. The fire took hold in a pile of acrylic fleece blankets. It's spread from there but the bed's iron, the rug's wool, the bed had woollen blankets on and it's mostly the fumes from acrylic we've been dealing with.'

'Then there's no harm…'

'There nearly was a hell of a lot of harm,' the chief said. 'The fire went up the curtains into the ceiling and there's insulation there that's melted. The house is choked with poisonous fumes. I've sent my men to clear the seat of the fire but they're all using breathing gear. Thank God for smoke alarms.'

And for Dom, Erin thought, stunned.

'How the hell did it start?' he asked. 'Do you know?'

There was no point in lying. No one was going to charge a six-year-old with criminal damage. She still had one of the fire-fighter's blanket draped around her but she was shivering. The last thing she wanted to do was stand and answer questions, but if this man didn't get the information he wanted from her he'd have to ask Dom, and all Dom's attention was needed now.

'Hell, those kids…' the firefighter said when she'd told him. 'They'll be the death of him.'

'You've met them?'

'A couple of their predecessors,' the man said grimly. 'Doc takes on the kids no one else will touch. He and Tansy...' He paused. 'That's right, she's away at her sister's. She'll have Doc's guts for garters when she comes back. A right little mother she makes. She and Doc are a great pair.'

That didn't sound good.

Um...what was she thinking? Fire, life-threatening peril, and here she was wondering about the unknown Tansy.

Around them the firefighters were moving in what seemed organised chaos. There were firefighters everywhere. A team was concentrating on the bedroom on the upper left of the house, but others were uncoiling what looked like a vast vacuum hose.

'What's that?'

'A suction tube,' the man told her. 'We'll get the burned stuff out of the house. We'll check the roof, put any last embers out, then start sucking out smoke.'

'Tonight?'

'Straight away. The smoke causes the most damage. And if I know Doc he'll want to stay here. He always does. He hates farming his kids out.'

'You mean this has happened before?'

'One of his kids stabbed him once,' the man said, watching the vacuum hose disappear inside the front door. 'Doc needed fifteen stitches but he wouldn't go to hospital. Nor would he let the cops take the kid away. The lad was only eight. The cops called us 'cos he'd locked himself in his room and was threatening to set the place on fire, but by the time we got here Doc had talked him out and was hugging him. Blood and all. Can you believe that? The kid's been reunited with his mother now and last I heard was doing okay. He and his mum still visit. Lots of Doc's kids still do.'

'How many?' Erin said faintly.

'God knows,' the man said. 'All I know is that he and Tansy

are heroes. I wish to hell we could get another doctor for the town so he had more time to spare. Now, if you'll excuse me, miss, I need to suck smoke.'

'I wish to hell we could get another doctor for the town so he had more time to spare...'

This was not the time to be thinking career moves. But the tiny idea had seeded itself already. The firefighter's words made it grow.

Her shoes were fine. As was Nathan's egg and Martin's pogo stick. Two hours later the house still stank of smoke but it was deemed no longer dangerous. The bedroom where Martin had lit the fire—Tansy's room—would need major work, but with its door not only closed but sealed so no smell could escape, the house started seeming like home again.

Dom had fielded twenty offers of accommodation that she'd heard, but she'd given up counting.

He'd knocked them all back.

'Once the smoke is clear we'll get back inside,' he explained. 'It'll be better for the kids not to move.'

Dom must be feeling weak at the knees himself, Erin thought as she watched him deflect offers, but he wasn't putting Martin down. The little boy was slumped on his shoulder. Erin wasn't sure whether he was asleep or not, but every time the voices round them rose, she saw Dom's arm round him tighten.

With his other hand he held Nathan. He didn't let them go, once.

'We're home here,' he said, over and over, trying to make his voice normal. 'The smoke makes everything seem worse than it is. But we're fine.'

And gradually the chaos became order. The onlookers melted into the night. Two of the fire engines left. One would stay.

'I know you wish us to the devil,' the fire-chief told Dom as they carried the kids back into the almost-normal living room. 'But the fire spread to part of the ceiling and there's no guarantee we haven't miss spots. There'll be two men staying upstairs all night, and there'll be more outside. Yes, you can stay in the house but you'll do so with our presence. Like it or leave it.'

Dom could see the sense. He smiled, rueful. 'Fine by me, Graham. We'll sleep round you.' He looked across at Erin. 'How about you? Can I accept any of these offers of help on your behalf?'

The locals were leaving, but he only had to call one back, say, 'Do you mind looking after Erin?' and she'd be away.

'No,' she said fiercely, involuntarily.

'No?'

She coloured. 'I… If it's okay with you. I might be able to help…with Marilyn.'

'That's right, we still have Marilyn,' he said, and he smiled, and she was reminded of that chuckle all over again.

'She's having the world's worst birth experience in dog history,' she said, and tried to make her voice not wobble. 'I'll settle her back by the fire.'

'If the very word doesn't make us all blench.'

'Fires are good,' she said, stoutly, aware that Martin's eyes had widened in alarm. 'Fires are lovely. This was an aberration.'

'What's an aberration?' Nathan said. He sounded exhausted. It was time he was tucked up into bed, wherever they could find a bed. But Erin knew that farming the kids out to strange beds tonight would be asking for trouble. Dom knew it and she knew it.

'An aberration's a mistake,' she said, meeting Dom's gaze full on. 'This was a little, smoky fire lit by mistake that made us all feel a bit sick. But there's a lovely fire in the kitchen stove and another in the living room. That's what we all want now. A lovely warm fire so I can get my cold toes warm.'

It was the right thing to say. They were wearing their night-wear plus blankets. Even though Erin had shoved on Dom's wellingtons over the dressings on her foot, her toes were freezing. So, it seemed, were everyone else's.

'Brilliant,' Dom, said and his eyes were giving her a message that said her approach had been right on all sorts of levels. 'It's what we all want. An ordinary fire to warm our toes. Let's get ourselves organised.'

It would take days before the stink cleared from the upstairs rooms, but downstairs the smoke had been sucked out before it had permeated enough to cause any damage. The windows were open, fresh air had blown through and it felt almost normal.

'So we're all sleeping downstairs,' Dom decided, and before they knew it burly firefighters had hefted mattresses and bedding downstairs and set up a row of beds in front of the sitting-room fire.

What had seemed a big room when Erin had had it to herself was now cramped. Three mattresses. Erin's divan.

Marilyn's mat.

'For she's not going to be the only one in the kitchen,' Erin decreed. 'One in, all in.'

'Fine by me,' Dom said.

The fire was still a pile of glowing embers in the grate. Dom added wood, building it up so it crackled and flared.

'Fire's great,' he said as Martin looked at it nervously. 'This is what fire's meant to do. Martin, I've been thinking. You've had a terrible experience—it should be useful for something. Tomorrow I'll teach you how to set and light a fire properly.'

Whatever Martin had been expecting it wasn't this. He even managed a sleepy smile.

Dom had set the beds so his was the closest to the fire, Martin's was next, then Nathan's and finally Erin's settee. So they were in a protective sandwich, two little boys with an adult on either side and Marilyn at their feet.

The kids were asleep in seconds. Erin knew she should sleep, too—but she could see Dom in the firelight. He was propped up on one elbow, looking over his charges. By the firelight she saw raw emotion playing on his face.

'I don't regret that kiss,' she said suddenly into the dark, and she saw him stiffen.

'Why aren't you asleep?'

'I'm watching you.'

'Don't.'

'Someone has to look out for you,' she said gently. 'You watch out for the whole world and no one watches out for you. Well, that's about to change. I don't regret that kiss one bit. It was a truly fabulous kiss. A kiss to dream about. You go to sleep now, Dominic Spencer, and know that tonight you're off duty. Responsibility's mine.'

'Right.'

'Believe it,' she whispered.

'You're shaking,' he said into the dark.

'I'm not.'

'I can hear it in your voice.'

Well, maybe she was. Somehow the events of the night had caught up with her.

'I'm okay.'

'You need a hug?'

'I might,' she said, cautiously.

'Why didn't you say so?' he said, and suddenly he was upright, stepping carefully across the sleeping boys, stooping to touch her face. And then, because there was no room to kneel by her bed in the crowded room—that surely must be the reason— he tugged back her blankets and slipped in beside her.

His arms came round her and held.

If she'd not been shaking before she was now. Or maybe...maybe not. It was a different sort of shaking.

'I needed to hold you,' he said.

'I...I know. I kinda need to be held,' she admitted.

'I know that, too. You were brilliant tonight.'

'You were, too.' She relaxed against him. Or sort of relaxed. Her back was curved into his chest. He was wearing pyjama bottoms but no top. She could feel his body through her silk pyjamas.

It certainly took a girl's mind off fire.

'I'm not seducing you,' he said, apropos of nothing in particular.

'No?' Her voice wasn't working properly. It sort of…squeaked.

'No,' he said, and she could feel his smile.

'Rats,' she whispered.

He chuckled—and held her closer. 'Hey, if I could I would, but how Mom and Pop Brady ever managed procreation with that lot…'

'I can't remember any combined Bradys,' she said cautiously, savouring the warmth of him against her. Loving the warmth of him against her. 'There was a His Bunch and Her Bunch and then no more.'

'Kids,' he said darkly. 'They're a contraceptive device second only to a brick wall.'

Right. Or not right. She wasn't sure. The feeling of his body against her was doing all sorts of strange things. Wonderful things. 'You…you want to tell me why you're in my bed, then?'

'To stop you shivering.'

'I think I've stopped shivering.'

'I'll be the judge of that. Besides, I need to thank you. You saved our lives tonight.'

'You saved yourselves.'

'I never would have got Martin downstairs without your help.' His voice was still hoarse from smoke inhalation. He sounded serious suddenly, and husky, and so damned sexy he was making her toes curl. 'I couldn't say it in front of the boys but I know how close we came to losing him,' he whispered into her ear. 'Thank you.'

'Hey, any time,' she whispered—and then she thought Dom must have been even more terrified than she'd been. Just because he was a man, did that make him less needful of comfort?

Instinctively she twisted to face him and her arms came round to hold him, tight.

'It's okay, Dom,' she said, trying—not altogether successfully—to focus on him as a person and not as the body he came with. 'We're all okay. And I'm sure Martin won't do such a thing again.'

'He might.'

'Then you'll be there to help him,' she said stoutly. And then, because it was what was in her heart, she said what she most wanted to say. 'Dom, I want to help you.'

'You already did.'

'No, long term.' She swallowed. 'I could help here. If you let me.'

'You mean medically?'

'Of course.' The medical bit was only part of it, she thought, but instinct told her to start with the medical offer and move on. 'I could take so much off your shoulders. Here. In this community. There's so much work!'

'Here? Are you nuts?' They were lying entwined like long-term lovers. It felt right, though, she thought. It felt entirely, wonderfully natural. 'You've just got a new job,' he said.

A new job. She forced herself to focus. That's right, she had, too. Head of Emergency Medicine. In another world.

But she'd shifted worlds. This was her world now and there was no going back.

'I've just had another epiphany,' she retorted. 'In fact, I've had a week of epiphanies. The work you're doing here...I can't imagine how you cope. I can't imagine any greater honour than being permitted to help you.'

'Tansy helps me.'

It was like a slap. She closed her eyes. She felt ill.

She was still holding him. She didn't know how to stop holding him.

'Erin?' He shifted away from her and she felt like weeping. Okay, she was being overemotional here but it had been some night and he was making her feel...

'Erin?'

She opened her eyes again, cautiously. He'd pushed himself up on his elbows and was gazing down at her in the firelight. Rueful.

'I'm sorry,' he said. 'I didn't mean to sound so blunt. Tansy does help with the boys. Medically, though…yes, I am stretched. But you and I… No.'

'No?'

'No.'

'Because?'

She put her hands up to touch his face. This was the most important moment in her life. She knew it.

Did he know it, too?

'Because of this,' he said.

And he kissed her.

It was a different kiss this time. Their last kiss had been born of fear and exhaustion and relief, but those emotions had passed. The warmth of the room, the knowledge of two little boys sleeping safe and warm beside them, the peace of the drama past—and the warmth and comfort they were taking from each other—combined into one lovely whole. Suddenly it seemed so right, so inevitable, so…true.

Dom was kissing her and the pain his words had caused was gone. She was singing inside. Her Dom. They were safe and warm and at peace, and she was in the arms of the man she loved. She was floating, dreamlike, responding to his kiss with every fibre of her being.

Dom, she whispered in her heart. Dom.

What the hell was he doing?

He was kissing a woman as he'd never kissed one before.

He was needing a woman.

She was luscious under his hands, soft, yielding but wanton.

Wanton. The word played in the back of his brain, in the tiny section that was free to think anything at all. For now wasn't about thinking. It was about feeling, touching, tasting, all five senses awake, alive, tuned to this woman as he'd never been tuned to a woman before.

Wanton.

That was the way she was with him. He knew—in that part of his brain he hadn't seemed to possess until he'd met her—that wanton wasn't an adjective he'd ever hear applied to Erin. She was the good child, the compliant, clever daughter, the dutiful and faithful friend.

She'd done all she was supposed to in life—but right now she was pleasing herself.

She wanted him as desperately as he wanted her.

Every part of her was yielding. Her body was crushed against his, her breasts moulding deliciously against his chest, her mouth closed on his, her tongue…her tongue…

She tasted of salt and heat and want. She tasted of everything he'd ever dreamed of.

His kiss deepened and she matched him, demanding as much as she gave, willing him to want more.

His hands tugged her hard against him, his fingers cupping her butt in her silken pyjamas so she was pulled right against him. She was doing her own tugging.

He could do with her what he willed and he knew that she'd come.

She'd follow where he led, or she'd lead herself if he willed.

He should stop. He had to stop.

But he could no sooner tear himself away from her than he could fly. He felt as if a part of him that had been torn away at birth had miraculously come home.

Erin…

Her hair smelled of smoke.

Erin.

The fire crackled in the grate, a small hissing explosion. It caught him. Pulled him up.

No.

Hell, what was he doing?

* * *

He was hers. Whatever he'd ask of her in this moment she'd give. She could love him no more in the future than she did now.

He was her man. She was his woman and she'd come home. Dom.

This was a long, lingering kiss, deep and sweet and right. She clung to him and he held her close, savouring the kiss as she savoured it, deepening it as she deepened it. Tugging her closer. Closer.

Loving her as she loved him?

But… Maybe not. No!

For the fire had spat and hissed and he'd pulled away as she could never have pulled away. Now he was holding her at arm's length, gazing at her as one might gaze at a precious, unattainable thing. Something so far out of his reach it was a dream.

'What is it?' she whispered. 'Oh, Dom…'

'I just…meant to tell you…meant to show you why your offer is impossible.' His voice was shaken. Desperate. 'It's the most generous offer I've ever heard—to give up your city practice and come here. But there's this between us… There's this. I never meant it to go so far.'

'So?'

'I don't want it.'

'It seems to me,' she whispered, fingers of ice suddenly whispering their way round her heart, 'that you do want it. As much as I do.'

'No.'

'Why not?'

'You've been here for less than two days. This makes no sense.'

'It makes all the sense in the world.'

'No,' he said, more strongly now. 'You're sweet and smart and beautiful and I'm not about to take advantage.'

'Hey! Isn't that ever so slightly patronising?'

'Whatever. But it's true.' He kissed her again then, but lightly this time, holding himself rigidly under control. The drama of the night had unveiled his need, but he had himself back together.

He slipped from under her blankets and rose and she could have wept.

'I want to help,' she said, and if she sounded needy she couldn't help it.

'I can't accept.'

'You might have to accept,' she whispered. 'This community is too big for one doctor. You're doing what you have to. Maybe I am, too.'

He shook his head. 'Neither of us is making sense,' he said softly, and he stooped and touched her lightly on the lips. It was a feather touch. It was like a touch of farewell.

'Enough. This is crazy. It's dreams talking, not reality. Goodnight, Erin,' he whispered. 'Go to sleep. In the morning we'll be sane again.'

'But I won't be sane tomorrow,' she muttered rebelliously under her breath as he returned to his makeshift bed. 'I'm sane now. I'm feeling like I've been insane all my life and I've just woken up. I'm feeling like it's time to come home.'

She didn't say it out loud, but she meant it. Somehow she just had to convince Dom...

That love worked?

She had to convince Dom that what she felt was for ever.

She hardly slept. When the phone went at six it didn't get the chance to ring a second time before Erin was out in the hall to answer it.

There were still firemen in the house. One of the men—the fire-chief, Graham—had started down the stairs to answer it. He stopped when he saw her. She smiled, waved the receiver at him, and pulled the sitting-room door closed so as not to wake Dom and the boys.

'Doc?' On the end of the line, a man's voice sounded frantic. The terror of last night kicked in again. Just because last night's terror was gone, it didn't mean the world was a safe place for everyone.

'I'm a doctor,' she said, smoothly professional. 'How can I help?'

'But the doc—'

'We had a house fire last night,' she said, trying to sound like it was no drama. 'Dr Dom's taken up with his kids. I'm the doctor on call. Will you allow me to help you instead?'

There was a pause. Then a shattering sob. 'I've just woken up,' he managed. 'I think my wife's dead.'

It took all of two seconds to decide someone needed to go, and that someone should be her.

This was Dom's patient. In theory she should wake him. But she glanced back into the living room and all three boys were sleeping like the dead.

Martin had snuggled next to Dom during the night. Dom had his arm across the little boy's shoulders. The sight made her suddenly blink away tears.

She was almost…jealous. It was dumb, but there it was. These guys were a family, and she wanted to be a part of it.

At least she could give them this time. Which meant this was her call.

Quietly she asked the questions she needed to know.

The lady had been suffering from advanced metastatic cancer. Dom had been looking after her at home. Yes, Dom had said she might die, but surely not so soon…

She covered the receiver and talked to Graham, who'd been watching with concern from the landing. 'Is there someone who can take me to Hughie Matheson's house?'

'Sure thing. Is Enid dead, then? We thought it might be soon.'

So the town was expecting this death. More and more, she knew this was something she could deal with. Yes, it'd be better for Hughie if Dom was able to come, but right now triage said those little boys needed him more.

She'd stowed her clothes in the downstairs bathroom so she could have privacy when she dressed. That meant she didn't need to go back into the living room. Two minutes later she was dressed in jeans and a thick sweater—and Dom's boots again—and Graham was ushering her out of the house.

'Thank God you're here,' he said, stowing Dom's medical bag into the back of his truck. 'Doc's driving himself into the ground. You don't want to move here permanently, do you?'

'I might,' she said, and he came close to tripping over his feet as he climbed into the truck.

'You're kidding.'

'Maybe I'm not,' she said cautiously. But the idea was taking solid form.

Dom had said flatly it was impossible. Okay, living in the same house was impossible—she conceded that. But what he was doing with the kids was so worthwhile. If she could share his medical load...

'Everyone says you need two doctors.'

'We need half a dozen,' Graham told her. 'We've been advertising for ever.'

'So if I were to stay...'

'You'd never move in with him,' Graham breathed.

'I... No.' Dom had said they couldn't work together because of this 'thing' between them. But maybe they could. If they stayed apart.

Apart for as long as he wanted.

'I reckon our Tansy'd have something to say about that,' Graham said, grinning. 'But that means you'd be needing somewhere to live. What about old Doc's place?'

Whoa. Things were suddenly moving really fast, even for her newly formed resolutions.

The dawn light was just starting to edge over the horizon. Their truck was headed out of town on a bumpy road. Around them were open paddocks full of sleepy sheep.

How could she move here?

But Graham wasn't treating the suggestion as silly.

'Where's…old Doc's place?' she ventured.

'How about I take you there after we finish at Hughie's?' Graham said, warming to his theme. 'It's a bachelor pad—a tiny house attached to the building that used to be the hospital. The government closed the hospital when old Doc died. This doc says he can't open it again—he can't have inpatients without back-up. But old Doc's place is owned by the town and it's for medical staff. That'd mean you. Hell, with two doctors we might be able to open the hospital again. What d'yer reckon?'

'I reckon I need to think about it,' she said cautiously. 'I need to talk to Dom.'

'What's this got to do with Dom?' Graham said easily, chuckling. 'In my other life I run the local hotel. I'm head of the chamber of commerce, plus I'm shire president. If there's the possibility of an extra doctor for this place, I'm not letting you go. Consider yourself hired.'

Enid Matheson was indeed dead, peacefully in her own bed, dying in her sleep with her husband beside her.

'There's not a lot of women lucky enough to have this as their farewell,' Erin said gently as she checked all vital signs. Then, just as gently, she touched the lady's face in the gesture of farewell she always used. Working in Emergency in a big city hospital meant most of her farewells didn't seem as right as this one. Enid had been in her eighties. There were photographs all over the house—Enid and Hughie, with kids, dogs, grandkids, ribbons for prize bulls, certificates for prize fruit cakes… The house was a cosy, well-loved testament to a woman who had known how to make a home.

Erin thought fleetingly back to her parents' home, to the super-clean granite and stucco architectural statement her parents worked so hard over—and she was aware of a stab of envy.

Then she thought of the bikes and pogo stick and general chaos in Dom's yard and felt a stab of something else. The same but different.

But now wasn't about her, she thought as she finished her examination. Hughie was sitting at the kitchen table, his head in his hands, silently weeping.

She put on the kettle and found two mugs. Outside Graham would be waiting but he'd said, 'You're not to worry—there's others taking care of things back at Dom's place and I have all the time in the world. Hughie'll need you. I'll wait for as long as you need.'

So she took him at his word. In a while she'd do the official stuff—fill in the death certificate, organise an undertaker, ask Hughie who she should call.

But if he'd desperately wanted his family to be with him he'd have called them by now. It seemed he wanted a little time first, before the business of dealing with death began. Thanks to Graham, she could give it to him.

'Tell me about Enid,' she said softly, as she put a mug of hot, sweet tea in front of him. 'This house is lovely. I'm guessing she's been a wonderful woman.'

'She is,' the old farmer said brokenly, and looked through into the bedroom. 'She was.' He shook his head. 'You...you really want to hear about her?'

It was a plea, pure and simple.

'Yes, I do,' Erin said strongly, and surprised herself by the truth of what she'd said.

This was a facet of medicine she'd never thought about. Trained and working in city hospitals she'd never been in the position where...

Where patients could be friends, she thought suddenly, with a flash of insight. This Easter was really changing her perspective.

Up until now she'd thought that Dom was a self-sacrificing hero. Now, as she sat in front of the ancient kitchen stove and shared a second and then a third cup of tea and heard about Enid from the time she and Hughie had first met, she thought, No, it worked both ways.

She could do this. What's more, she *wanted* to do this.

'Doc's been great,' Hughie said, and she had to haul herself out of her own thoughts and back to him.

'He's looked after Enid well?'

'When we knew the cancer had spread, our kids said we should put her in a hospice. But Doc said if she wanted to stay home then stay home she would, and he's moved heaven and earth to keep her here. He's been here nearly every day. He brings those kids with him—I take 'em for a ride on the tractor while he looks after Enid. You know, she's hardly had pain at all. The minute there's pain you ring me, he says, and we do…we did…and he'd be here. He's one in a million. But he works too hard.'

'I know that,' she said. 'I'm thinking of helping him.'

The old farmer's gaze lifted from the dregs of his tea. His eyes were red-rimmed from weeping but he looked at her now—he really looked.

'That'd be great,' he said simply. 'You're such a one as he is. I can see it sticking out a country mile. And now…' He took a deep breath.

'And now?'

'It's time to call the kids,' he said. 'It's time to call the church and the funeral chaps. Thank you for giving me this time, miss. I've appreciated it more than you can say.'

'You want me to make the calls for you?'

'If you would,' he said with dignity. 'I'll sit with Enid until they come.'

Afterwards Graham drove her home past the old doctor's house and the building that had once been Bombadeen's hospital. Weirdly it still looked neat and freshly painted—a long, low building of rendered brick surrounded by well-tended gardens and ancient eucalypts.

'It looks like it closed yesterday,' Erin said, confused.

'The locals hated it when it closed,' Graham told her. 'A few of the oldies have taken it on as their retirement project. If we can ever attract another doctor to the place, we can get it open again in a trice.'

'I'd imagine there'd be heaps of bureaucracy.'

'I'm really good at bureaucracy.' Graham was casting her thoughtful, sideways glances.

'Dom probably likes being the only doctor.'

'Are you kidding?'

'If I moved here...'

'You really are interested?' He frowned. 'Miss...Doc...if you don't mind me saying, I'm hearing you've only been here for two days. It's your car that's at the bottom of the Boulder Creek Road. Maybe you hit your head on the way down. I don't think you should make your mind up quite yet.'

'That's generous of you.'

'It is, isn't it?' he said cheerfully, and drew the truck into the hospital yard. 'Okay, I've given you my obligatory warning. Now let's introduce you to your new home. That dog of yours is going to love this yard.'

'Right.'

He pulled to a halt. She thought he was about to get out but instead he hesitated again. 'You know, I shouldn't say this but I have daughters of my own. You and Dom...'

'What about me and Dom?'

'He's a really attractive man, miss,' he said cautiously. 'My daughters tell me he's what they call a hunk. You're not imagining yourself in love with him after two days.'

'No!' Yes.

'That's alright, then,' he said, glad to have that cleared up. 'My daughters say there's Tansy and only Tansy. The local lasses have thrown everything they can at him but no one succeeds. And now you…' He shook his head. 'Okay, I'm talking out of turn. I know it. I've said my piece and now I'll shut up. Now, let's go show you your new home.'

They were at the kitchen table eating cornflakes when she got back. And Easter eggs.

'Happy Easter,' Dom said. 'The Easter Bunny's been.'

They all had an egg in front of them. Or half an egg. There'd obviously been considerable egg consumption in her absence.

But at the end of the table was an empty place, neatly set. In the middle of the place-mat was a shiny, pink-foiled egg.

A tiny white flag was stuck in the top. 'Erin,' it said.

Erin. It was *her* egg.

Weirdly it made tears prick at the back of her eyes. In all this chaos, Dom had still found time to play Easter Bunny.

And he'd remembered her. This very girly pink egg must have been deliberately organised. For her.

'The Easter Bunny's more reliable than the chap who cooks the Easter buns,' he said, and smiled at her with that drop-dead smile that had her heart doing back flips.

'You bought me an egg.' Dammit, her bottom lip was quivering.

'The bunny brought you the egg,' Nathan corrected her. 'They were on the table when we woke up this morning.'

'The bunny's good,' she managed.

'How do you think he knew you were here?' Nathan asked.

'Magic,' she said, and sat down because she needed to. They were gorgeous—the three of them. Her boys…

Now, that was a dumb, possessive thing to think. These guys had nothing to do with her. Though Dom might end up being her partner.

Her medical associate. Nothing more.

She had to get her bottom lip under control.

'Where have you been?' Dom asked, passing the cornflakes. 'The fire guys said you had a call.'

'Can I eat my egg before I tell you?'

'If you must.'

'Of course I must,' she said, and unwrapped her egg—quite a big egg actually. She bit a very satisfactory hole in the pointy end, munched for a bit, then placed her egg, hole-side down, in front of her cereal bowl. Then she poured her cornflakes.

'That looks like a ritual,' Dom said.

She nodded. 'I've done it every Easter Sunday for as long as I can remember. One year the Easter Bunny brought me a chocolate rabbit instead of an egg. It messed with my psyche all year.'

'I imagine it did,' Dom said faintly. 'So where have you been?'

'Out to the Mathesons'.'

He was half way through handing her the milk jug. His hand froze in mid-air.

'What—?'

'A lovely peaceful ending,' she said, and smiled across the table at him. 'Thanks to you. Well done, Dr Spencer.'

'Hughie rang?'

'At six. Graham drove me out there.'

'You should have woken me.' There was no mistaking the anger—a flash of fury.

'Right,' she said. 'You copped more smoke than me last night. I decided this morning that you're my patient and it was me making the decisions.'

'You had no right.'

'I know,' she said softly. 'And, indeed, if there was anything you could have done I would have woken you. But there was nothing.'

'Can we talk about it later?' he said, tightly.

She thought, Uh-oh, she'd acted unprofessionally. She'd stepped in and acted in his stead without a by-your-leave.

'Of course we can.'

But then she looked at the little boys oscillating between egg and cornflakes and she knew she'd done the right thing. They'd woken to find Dom beside them. They needed him today.

Dom had made the decision to be a foster-parent. He had to accept the consequences.

What she was thinking must have been obvious. The tight lines of anger changed to something else—confusion?

'What, not prepared to take an official reprimand?' he asked, but his heart didn't sound like it was in it.

'Not for Enid,' she said, and tilted her chin. 'Or for anything else I may have done this morning.'

His voice grew apprehensive. 'What the hell else have you done this morning?'

She peeped a smile at him. It was Easter Sunday after all, a good day, a day for celebration. Dom looked grim and tired and he was getting help whether he needed it or not.

'I've found a home for Marilyn,' she told him. 'But discussion's for after breakfast. If you'll excuse me, I have an Easter egg to concentrate on.'

He needed to get his head in order.

The drama of the night was still close to overwhelming. He'd nearly lost Martin.

He'd taken his mind off the game, he thought grimly. These boys needed so much attention. He couldn't afford to be distracted. And Erin was definitely…distracting.

She was lovely. And that kiss last night…

He'd gone to sleep with that kiss lingering in his senses. He felt it still. She'd kissed him as if she'd meant it, as if she wanted to be a part of him.

Well, that was a crazy thought.

Or maybe not so crazy. He had a great home, a great job, and he had… Yeah, okay, he had enough going in the testosterone stakes to make him interesting. Ruby had told him that over and over. 'You'll make some lucky girl a lovely husband. Just because your parents were a disaster it doesn't mean the rest of the world's damaged. Relationships do work. Open yourself up and some nice girl will slip right in.'

While he wasn't looking. That's what this felt like—as if Erin had slipped in while his back had been turned. And now she was in and he couldn't take his mind off her. If she hadn't been here maybe he'd have sensed that Martin had been troubled last night.

He couldn't stay this preoccupied. He had to get her out of here.

He'd promised she could stay over Easter.

'You needn't worry. I'm organising myself alternative accommodation,' she said, and smiled sweetly. He blinked. Were his thoughts so obvious?

'Where?'

'I'll tell you after breakfast,' she repeated. 'Now, if you don't mind, I haven't eaten enough egg.'

CHAPTER TEN

ONLY, of course, after breakfast things got busy. Really busy.

For a start there was the little matter of a fire having almost destroyed a bedroom and part of the ceiling. It seemed Easter Sunday was no reason why the fire department couldn't come out in force. The morning ended up as an endless parade of men in hard hats traipsing up and down the stairs, climbing ladders, knocking holes in roofing tiles and clambering about the ceiling.

'It's still structurally sound,' Graham somewhat grudgingly admitted at lunchtime. 'But you've got your work cut out getting Tansy's room ready for her to come home.'

'I need to contact her and find out what she wants done with her damaged possessions,' Dom said. 'We'll keep as much as possible intact until she comes back.'

'When will she be back?'

'In a couple of weeks,' Dom said, as Erin listened from behind. The unknown Tansy.

She shouldn't mind, Erin thought. Why did the idea of Tansy have the power to unsettle her?

She knew exactly why, but she was trying hard not to admit it.

Luckily she had a distraction. A couple of church ladies arrived and offered to take the boys on an Easter-egg hunt.

Even though the thought of the hunt was enticing, the boys were clingy and Martin still needed observation. An X-ray had shown a rib had a hairline crack, though it didn't seem to be bothering him. But the boys wanted to go. Dom was needed at the house, so Erin offered to go with them.

The hunt was in a patch of bushland behind the church. Erin limped about on the sidelines as the boys hunted, wishing Dom could be there, trying not to think that he'd seemed relieved when she'd suggested taking the boys—and thus herself—away.

She watched, and while she did so she took stock of this community, wondering whether she could do what Graham had proposed that morning.

But from everyone she told she was a doctor, she got the same response.

'You wouldn't like to practise here, would you? We're desperate for another doctor. And it'd be wonderful to get the hospital up and running again.'

She could do good here. She could be needed.

She could be close to Dom.

No, no and no! The decision had to be made on its own merits. Dom had Tansy. Tansy gave him all the help at home he needed. He didn't want or need anyone else…personally. This had to be a professional proposition only.

So she needed to talk to Dom about it.

Last night he'd rejected it out of hand.

For dumb reasons, though, she thought. They were illogical reasons. He had to see sense.

It was a gorgeous day. The kids were whooping through the patch of bushland reserve where the church ladies had hidden eggs, the terrors of the night forgotten. They came tearing back every now and then to show her their finds, and she found herself absurdly touched.

'Erin, Erin, we've found nine. Ten. Eleven!'

Something about last night had bonded them to her. They trusted her.

What Dom was doing with these kids was great. Fantastic. He had to let her help.

* * *

He missed her.

She and the kids were gone for three hours. It gave him a chance to get some order into the house. A group of church ladies had taken themselves off egg-hunt duties and arrived with mops and brooms. They went through the house like a dose of salts, and by the time they'd finished, the place was cleaner than it had been before the fire.

All the time they worked they chattered. And asked questions about Erin.

'She seems lovely,' he was told as the ladies worked. 'We gather she was lovely this morning. Hughie's daughter said she sat with him for over an hour. She made him cups of tea and listened for as long as he wanted to talk. She didn't rush him at all, and that's after she'd crashed her car and hurt her foot and all. You should have told us, Doc. We'll organise the men to pull the car up from the river. Doesn't matter that it's Easter. What sort of doctor is she? She doesn't want a job, does she? Ooh, I wonder what Tansy will think of her?'

They were about to find out.

At four o'clock four cars pulled up outside the house almost simultaneously. Dom was in his surgery, dusting through a pile of patient notes. The women had cleaned in here but patient confidentiality demanded he do this himself.

The sound of the kids' voices made him look out the window.

Erin and the kids were being dropped off by a lady he recognised as Marg Lalor, head of the church choir. That was surprising on its own. Marg was a nervy driver and she didn't like having passengers. She also Didn't Like Boys. For her to offer to drive Erin and the kids home was astonishing.

Pulling up behind them was a Porsche.

Charles. Great.

Then there was a taxi. Followed by a small, red car he thought he recognised. Ruby?

But… Ruby was in Dolphin Beach. His elderly foster-mother

had intended to celebrate Easter with his foster-brother Pierce and Pierce's new wife, Shanni.

Nope. Ruby was definitely here, tugging her battered overnight bag out of her car, beaming at the kids.

'Martin. Nathan. I hear you and your dad have been having some excitement. And Tansy…'

For it was Tansy, looking hot and bothered, edging out of the taxi, dropping her purse, swearing, dropping her shawl, finally sitting down on the kerb, opening her purse and emptying its contents onto the grass.

'I swear I've got a fifty-dollar note. Maybe I can do it in coins. Can you wait for a bit?'

And in the middle of it all…Erin, looking confused.

Uh-oh. He grabbed his wallet and went to confront his…family?

'Tansy!'

There was no mistaking the joy in the little boys' voices.

The woman sitting on the kerb counting coins looked like…well, maybe like a Tansy ought to look, Erin thought. She was tall and buxom. She'd made an attempt to subdue her copper-red hair into a knot but there was no way hair like that could be subdued. Half her hair was in the knot, the rest was a mass of frizzy curls. She was wearing a ragged-edged purple skirt that reached her bright red boots. Her lacy blouse was cut low, a mass of bright red beads wound round her neck and—until she'd dropped it in the dust—she'd also been wearing a shawl. Daffodil yellow.

She looked maybe mid-thirties?

She was gorgeous!

Why Erin's heart should sink at the sight of her… Well, why shouldn't it? She was so far gone she no longer had the strength to lie to herself.

Tansy was beautiful. She minded.

The boys launched themselves at Tansy from a distance and coins went everywhere.

She abandoned the money. She hugged the boys as if they belonged to her. 'I'm so pleased to see you guys,' she said. 'Mrs Neale rang me at sparrow's f— at rooster crow this morning and said you were in trouble. It's taken me three flights and all day to get here.'

Erin had just alighted from the car. Marg—the lady from the church—was talking to her.

She wasn't listening. She was watching Tansy's flaming red curls bent over two small heads, and she was aware of such a jab of jealousy it was like a physical pain.

Tansy was back now. Things would be fine. Dom could go back to work; there was no need for her to stay.

'Oi.' The call came from a dumpy little woman dressed in twinset, pearls and neat, sensible skirt and shoes. She was standing in the road beside a big, canvas holdall. She was watching Tansy and the kids with approval. 'Don't I get a hello?'

'Ruby,' the kids yelled, and abandoned Tansy and careered round the far side of the taxi to reach her.

'Can I get paid?' the taxi driver said—plaintively—and Erin was suddenly aware of Charles approaching from behind. He had his wallet out, was counting notes, waving away change—that was such a Charles thing to do—and was moving to help Tansy to her feet.

'Hi,' Tansy said. 'Who are you?'

'Charles,' he said easily, smiling down at her. 'And you?'

'I'm Tansy.'

Charles did have a nice smile, Erin thought as she watched them. He hardly used it on her any more. He was too busy improving her—or disapproving of her. But when he smiled…

He was smiling at Tansy now. And Tansy was smiling at him. Charles seemed…dumbstruck.

'Find any eggs?'

She turned and Dom was behind her. He was watching the Charles-Tansy tableau, but his hand came down on her shoulder and rested, just briefly, as if he knew there was a certain amount of emotion here she didn't know what to do with.

'Seventeen,' she said absently. 'We've eaten six.'

'Well done, you.'

'It seems we have the cavalry,' she said, cautiously.

'We do indeed.' He didn't shift his hand and she was irrationally grateful.

'Tansy and Charles…and Ruby?'

'My foster-mother. I might have known she'd be here.'

'Why?'

'There was a fire last night,' he said, sounding half fond, half exasperated. 'Ruby and Tansy have the same fine-tuned antennae. It's a wonder the firefighters beat them here. And Charles…why do you think he's here?'

'I've come to take you home,' Charles said, dragging his eyes from Tansy with what looked like difficulty. 'We heard the doctor's house burned down last night. It was on the local news. Erin, you need to be sensible.'

'I don't,' Erin muttered, but maybe she did.

'You don't have anywhere to stay.'

'But it isn't burned down,' Tansy said, turning to survey the house. 'I was expecting much worse. But, hey, is that my bedroom window boarded up?'

'Your bedroom's burned,' Dom said.

'I lit the fire,' Martin said in a scared little voice, and any doubt Erin had that Tansy was a Very Nice Person dissipated just like that. Tansy hauled the little boy into her arms, gave him a hug that looked as if it could have cracked more ribs and kissed the top of his head.

'I imagine it must have been a mistake,' she said. 'Has Dom talked to you about it?'

'Y-yes.'

'Then there's nothing more to be said.'

'So you don't need me.' Ruby, too, was staring at the house

like it had betrayed her. 'I thought you might like me to take the boys back to Dolphin Bay.'

'The boys are fine,' Dom said.

'So…can I still stay the night?' she asked. 'I can't turn round and drive all the way back. Can we all sleep here?'

'Um…maybe not,' Dom said. 'The boys' bedroom is okay, and mine is, too, but Tansy's isn't, and Erin's using the sitting room.'

'I've come to take Erin home,' Charles said, but he was sounding less sure of himself now. He was still watching Tansy. Mesmerised. 'Maybe we can even take the dog,' he added, like it was a rehearsed speech. 'In view of the fire, my mother says it's the only Christian thing to do.'

Tansy snorted. Why hadn't *she* snorted? Erin thought, and jealousy returned in force.

The snort threw Charles off balance. He really was a good person, Erin thought again. He'd been put under as much pressure by their combined parents as she had. *'Do the right thing by Erin…'*

He was a good person but she didn't want to marry him. Especially not now. Not when she'd figured what she could feel.

Dom's hand was still on her shoulder. It felt weird. It felt…right. For she needed determination, and if Dom's hand on her shoulder gave her that determination, well and good.

Okay. Deep breath and jump.

'You don't need to take me home,' she said, to Charles and to all of them. She took a deep breath and managed a smile. 'And of course Ruby can stay. I have alternative accommodation. I've figured it out. I'm taking a new direction and I may as well tell you all. I'm taking a job as a local doctor. Charles, my home is here.'

If she'd detonated a bomb she could hardly have had less of an impact. They stood, stunned, all of them, staring at her like she'd grown two heads.

She couldn't see Dom. He was behind her. She was aware that his hand had stiffened on her shoulder.

She should have told him first. Of course she should. But she already knew his misgivings and she'd decided to ignore them.

Maybe those misgivings were valid and maybe they weren't. She could always leave. But, dammit, she was going to try. Surprise is the essence of attack, she thought. She needed to breach defences she knew instinctively were all around the man standing behind her.

Maybe that was a dumb thing to think when Tansy was here. Maybe Tansy had already breached his defences. But Dom still had his hand on her shoulder. If he and Tansy were an item, surely he'd have let her go by now. He and Tansy... Maybe not.

Please not.

She needed a smile. She needed...something. She looked round and found Ruby had the required smile. It was a smile of questions but it was a smile nonetheless.

'You're moving in with my son?'

'Dom's your son?'

'My foster-son,' Ruby said, extricating herself from kids and moving forward. She gripped Erin's hands, kissed her warmly on the cheek, then set her aside and hugged Dom as if he were the same age as Martin and Nathan.

She reached about as high as his chest.

'You've found a woman,' she said, sounding delighted.

'No,' Dom said adamantly, and Erin thought maybe it behoved her to clear a few things up.

'I'm not moving in with Dom.'

'You're not?' Ruby said, sounding disappointed.

'I'm moving into the old doctor's house by the hospital.'

'You're kidding,' Dom said—faintly.

'But that's wonderful,' said the church lady. In all the excitement she had been forgotten. 'I'm so glad. I'll get Graham to get the contracts drawn up straight away. And seeing you're tight for accommodation here, I'll organise to set the old doctor's house up so you can sleep there tonight. We'll even supply dog food.' She beamed. 'Nothing like striking while the iron's hot, don't you think?'

'Huh?' said Charles, and he said it for all of them. 'Huh' was right.

'Bye,' the church lady said, and climbed back into her car and drove off.

One down, Erin thought, dazed. Many more to go.

She needed to get Dom alone.

Like that was going to happen.

It happened.

'I'll drive you there now,' Dom said, sounding suddenly grim.

She thought 'Huh' again, even if she didn't say it.

'You can't,' she said. 'Everyone's here.'

'Which is why I need to be somewhere else. Charles, can you help Tansy and Ruby inside with their things? You girls can have the two usable upstairs bedrooms. The boys and I will keep sleeping in the sitting room. Erin, I'll take you—'

'And Marilyn,' she said.

'And Marilyn,' he agreed, sounding goaded.

'Erin…' Charles said.

'They want to be alone,' Tansy said unexpectedly, and tucked her arm confidingly in his. 'I can sense these things.'

'You're good,' Ruby said warmly. 'A woman after my own heart. Charles, can you take this holdall?'

'Erin…'

'Charles, tell our parents I love them,' Erin said, but she had to speak fast for Dom had her hand and was leading her forcibly back to the house. 'I'll ring them tonight. And thank you for coming to rescue me but I think I might have rescued myself. Dom, where are we going?'

'To fetch your dog, of course,' Dom said. 'And your toothbrush. And then to get rid of at least one woman from my life.'

CHAPTER ELEVEN

THEY hardly spoke until she was in the front seat of Dom's car, and they were heading across town. Erin's belongings had been hastily stuffed into her overnight bag. Marilyn was on the back seat, looking as confused as a bulldog could look. No woman in a maternity suite had ever been shuffled between so many beds, but as long as her head count of pups was correct she seemed resigned.

Erin didn't feel resigned. She felt breathless, and a little afraid.

Dom looked downright furious.

They reached the centre of town, drove past the fire station and a couple of volunteers were still there. They got cheery waves. Erin waved back.

Dom didn't wave.

'Are you going to tell me what you're playing at?' he said at last, tightly, and she stared at the road in front of her and thought of what she needed to say.

'I guess…this was a spur-of-the-moment decision. To work here.'

'You're not serious.'

'I think I am.'

'You want what, a nice idyllic home in the country.'

'That's not what I'm looking for,' she said evenly. 'I need…to be needed. I don't want to be needed to play violin like my brother and sister. I don't want to marry Charles to make our parents happy. I want to do something for me.'

'And Bombadeen's supposed to provide it?'

'I think it can,' she said evenly. 'I don't know, of course. I'll have to wait and see.'

'So you'll walk away from your job. Leave your employer in the lurch…'

'That's not fair. I'm about to start a new job heading our emergency department. I won the job by a whisker over two other doctors who are still available. I'm on two weeks' leave before starting. That means there's heaps of time for another applicant to be delighted that I can no longer take up the appointment.'

'You have all the answers.'

'You mean you don't want me?'

The question was tossed into the air like a hand grenade. They drove in stillness, waiting for it to explode.

It didn't. But neither did it disappear.

'So what are you proposing?' he asked at last, sounding strained.

'That I live in the old doctor's house and practise medicine. I can at least give it a few weeks' trial. Every single person I talked to today told me how overworked you are. They say non-urgent stuff has to go to Campbelltown because you can't handle it. Is that right?'

'Yes, but—'

'So I wouldn't be setting up in opposition to you. I'd be sticking up a sign saying I'm here for Doc Dom's leftovers.'

'My leftovers.'

'I'll even do insurance medicals,' she promised grandly. A greater offer she couldn't make. Insurance medicals were renowned for being the bane of a doctor's life. In the midst of a busy day they took an hour of crossing t's and dotting i's.

How could he help but be impressed? And he was. 'You're kidding,' he murmured. And then—amazingly—he smiled.

Great. That's what she'd been aiming for. It was starting to seem like a reasonable career ambition—to make Dom smile.

She smiled back and the tension lessened. A little.

'You're a top doctor,' he said cautiously, as if he was thinking it through. 'You'd never have got to head the emergency medicine team if you weren't good.'

'I do a nifty line in sticky plasters,' she said, and looked hopeful.

'And the rest,' he said. His smile died. He was serious again but the tension was gone. 'You'll have skills I can't guess at. But why? For this decision to come out of nowhere…'

'See, that's where you're wrong,' she said, and suddenly she knew she only had to tell the truth. Sure, there was her very definite attraction to this man, but the moment she'd thought of taking on this job things had settled that had been jumbled for a very long time.

'I loved this morning,' she told him. She clasped her hands together on her knees and hoped he got it.

He got it. 'Spending time with Hughie…'

'It felt right,' she said. 'Working in a city emergency department, I've lost count of the times I've had to face death. But this morning…instead of leaving Hughie with a social worker, I made a cup of tea and sat down and talked. It felt…right.'

'It's why I'm here,' he said simply. 'I've never want to be anything but a family doctor.'

'My family might see it as failure,' she told him. 'But it's not. I saw it clearly this morning. And then I thought if I have to move apartments anyway—I can't have Marilyn in my hospital flat and there's no way I'm giving her up—why not move here? I know you have misgivings about us but I think—I hope—we can work it out. I want to give it a try.'

'You're serious?'

'I am.'

It seemed he couldn't think of anything else to say.

Two minutes later they reached the house. Two women were

carrying in armloads of bedding. An elderly man in overalls was carrying in…a dog kennel?

'My God,' Dom said. 'This *is* serious. I knew Marg's organising skills were good, but this…'

'I don't think Marilyn's ready for a kennel,' Erin said, looking dubious. 'I sort of see her at the end of my bed. This…this is happening very fast.'

'It surely is,' he said drily. 'You'll wake up tomorrow and this'll seem like some crazy aberration.'

'Maybe.' But she didn't think so. She climbed from the car and went to retrieve her dog. But Dom was before her.

'I'll carry Marilyn. You bring the puppies.'

'This is your last move, Marilyn,' she told the dog and Marilyn looked up at her with a mournful expression that said she didn't believe it for a minute.

Erin followed Dom into the house. Inside a mini working bee had begun. They were greeted with good-hearted cheer and the guy with the dog kennel took one look at Marilyn and swore.

'Sheesh, Doc, there's no way that butt will go through this opening.'

He was talking to her, Erin realised. She'd just become…Doc.

She smiled, but absently. She walked through the little house, carrying puppies, while Dom and Marilyn followed behind.

The house looked like it had been built back in the 1920s. Heavy oak wainscotting, diamond-patterned windows with thick, irregular glass. Heavy furniture, well used. Lots of leather, worn carpets, a fireplace in the front room already set for lighting.

The afternoon sun was glinting through the panes of glass, throwing diamonds all across the room.

She pushed open the door into the kitchen. An ancient cooker took up half the far wall. The same diamond-patterned windows were on either side of the cooker. This room, though, faced east, and through the windows… The sea.

'It's fabulous,' she breathed. She'd seen it briefly that morning but now the sun was out it was amazing.

'We put locums up here,' Dom said. 'When we can get them. It only has one bedroom.'

'Marilyn and I only need one bedroom.' Everyone was looking at her—men and women who'd moved heaven and earth in record time to get this place looking inviting, she realised. There was a basket of bread, fresh made and smelling wonderful, on the kitchen bench. There was a box of groceries on the table. A big bunch of crimson poppies was scattered in a blue striped jug on the dresser.

'Home,' she breathed.

'It's blackmail,' Dom muttered. 'How do you think they got me here?'

'The same route?'

'The job was advertised, I came here for an interview and met Tansy. She was on the hospital board. She showed me this house. I said I fostered kids, and needed room for kids and a house-keeper. Tansy took me on a tour of the town, stopped to give me a coffee at the local café and before I'd finished my coffee, the locals had my house set up. I was taken to the house I'm in now. Same deal. Even the same bread.' He grinned at a white-haired old gentleman out in the passage. 'Pete makes the best bread in the district. And Tansy was part of the package.'

'Tansy…'

'"You take a job here, you get to eat this bread, you get to live in this house and here's your housekeeper," I was told. With their marketing strategies I couldn't believe the town had been without a doctor for ten years.'

'But have they worked?' It was Graham, standing at the back of the pack of onlookers. 'Do we have another doctor?'

'I think so,' Erin whispered, though she already knew the answer.

'Go away, the lot of you,' Dom said, shaking his head in ex-asperation. 'The lady's crashed her car and is stuck. I'm not taking advantage of her.'

'You're more of a gentleman than I am, then,' Pete said, and cackled.

'We need to talk medicine,' Dom retorted. 'Enough of the salesmanship. You've made your point. Leave the lady to me.'

'As long as you keep her,' Pete retorted, and looked Erin up and down in absolute approval. ''Cos the rest of us can see she's a keeper. Graham, let's go chop a mutt-sized butt-hole out of this kennel.'

They were left alone. Standing in the perfect little kitchen, looking at each other.

Dom was still holding Marilyn. Erin was still holding pups.

First things first. Dom set Marilyn down, disappeared into the bedroom and came back with a pile of blankets.

'They're old,' he told Erin. 'We set the bed up with duvets for the locum. There's more than enough to spare for Marilyn.'

So they set up a bed for Marilyn, beside the stove, in a corner of the kitchen where she'd be out of the way. The morning sun would stream in on her. The back door was at hand.

'If you stay I could chop a dog flap in the door,' Dom said, sounding reluctant.

'I'm staying.'

'You don't know that yet.'

'I do know it.' She was arranging the pups on the blanket, showing each of them to Marilyn in turn. 'There you go, sweetheart, all your babies are present and correct. This is your permanent home. I'll paint a sign on the wall if you like—"Marilyn Sleeps Here".'

'I'll show you our hospital. If you really mean it.'

'I mean it.'

'You're not doing it because…' He hesitated, and then suddenly he swore. 'I should never have kissed you.'

'Maybe I should never have kissed you.' Wrong, her heart said, but she had some pride.

'Anyone I work with…it has to be purely professional.'

She put her hands on her hips. 'So why wouldn't it be professional?'

'I have no idea,' he said, sounding goaded. 'Or maybe I do.'

'So? Everyone says you're desperate for a partner. Do you like being the only doctor for miles?'

'No.'

'Then it's just this attraction thing.'

'Which is nonsense,' he snapped. 'Okay, so we get over it.' He turned away abruptly, heading out into the hall and then through a door to the side.

The door led to a hospital in miniature. There was an office and four small wards, each with two beds. The beds weren't made up but the walls were painted in cheerful pastels. The green linoleum gleamed with polish. Dom led the way to a room at the rear and Erin found herself in a miniature theatre. It was big enough to perform not-so-minor surgery. The lights overhead were new and modern. The trolley under the lights looked ready to receive a patient right now.

'The old doc used to operate by himself,' Dom said. 'During the war he was the only doctor for a hundred miles. He'd take out an appendix all on his own.'

'And do a crossword on the side, I expect,' Erin said ruefully. 'Boy, do those old guys make us look pussycats. What do you use it for now?'

'Minor stuff—and I mean minor stuff. Certainly not an appendix. My surgery back home is too small, so I'm back and forth here, at need.'

'Will I get in the way?' she asked. 'If I'm in the background helping?'

'Look, Erin…'

'What?' She hitched herself up onto the examination couch and met his gaze straight on. 'Look, what?'

'You can't really be serious.'

'Of course I'm serious. This place is fantastic. Graham tells me this place is desperate for a doctor; he's shire president and he's offered me a contract. It seems just what I'm looking for, except the current incumbent—which would be you—looks like he has a mouthful of sour grapes.'

'I do not.'

'You certainly do,' she said. 'If you're worrying about my qualifications, they're excellent, and Graham says the district's so desperate if I was three-quarters dead and three-quarters drunk they'd still be interested.'

'You know I'm not looking for a relationship,' he said flatly, and she almost fell off the couch.

'Excuse…excuse me?' she tried to say—but it turned into a choking cough. He was watching her from the far side of the room like she was a ticking bomb.

It took her a couple of minutes to recover. He didn't move.

'Some doctors,' she said at last, when she could finally talk, 'would have fetched their patients a glass of water when that happened. Especially after last night. I might have impaired lung capacity from smoke inhalation.'

'If that's a possibility you'd better go home. With Charles.'

'Why do you want to get rid of me?'

'I told you. I'm not—'

'In the market for a relationship. I heard you. I'm here as a doctor, not a mistress.'

'You kissed me.'

'So I did, you big oaf,' she snapped. 'And you kissed me back. Last night was truly horrible and we were both terrified and we're all alive and I was so thankful that I would have kissed Marilyn. In fact, I seem to remember that I did kiss Marilyn.'

'Not like you kissed me.'

'Not being Marilyn, you'd know how?' she snarled, and he blinked.

'Um…'

'Look, let's get this on a professional basis and keep it there,' she snapped. 'I've been asked to work here as a doctor. I believe there's room for both of us in this town. Is there not?'

'I haven't advertised for help. You didn't ask—'

'I ought to have asked.'

'So you concede that at least?'

'Of course. But I'm desperate. I need a home for Marilyn.'

'She's not even your dog.'

'She is,' she said and swung off the examination couch and stood tall. 'Look, I've jolted you out of your comfort zone...'

'You haven't...'

'But I've been jolted further,' she snapped again. 'It was me who crashed into a river, who almost killed myself, who saved Marilyn, who helped save Martin, who spent all last night trying to figure how I could get my life back and suddenly realising I don't want it back. You're doing good in this town, Dominic Spencer, and I want to share it. How selfish is it of you not to let me?'

'Selfish...'

'Yes, selfish. This is a fantastic set-up. You're telling me I can't stay?'

'You'll be gone in a week.'

'I believe the contract Graham is drawing up is for six months. Am I so appalling?'

'No, but—'

'But what?' she demanded, exasperated. 'What's the worst that can happen? Graham tells me you have an outreach patient population of over eight thousand. Surely you can spare the odd patient or two. And if you're worried I might hit on you, surely you're old enough to fend me off. In fact, consider me fended.'

'I don't know whether I can work with you,' he said, goaded. 'Can't you understand that? The way I feel... How can I risk it? I need to stay as I am. My work's important to me. My kids are important to me. You mess with my head.'

'And you mess with mine. So maybe we need to sort it. Tell

me you're not the least bit interested in me, or you're in love with Tansy, or you swore celibacy until Armageddon. Just say it and then forget it. And I will, too. End of story. Professional colleagues and nothing more.'

He stared at her, seemingly baffled. She gazed calmly back.

The phone rang.

He didn't want her.

She watched him speak into the phone, as she saw his body tense and stay rigidly turned away from her…

I've lost, she thought bleakly. Where do I go from here?

'Where's the crash?'

Despite her confusion, despite feeling humiliated to her socks, she picked up on what he was saying.

'How many? Hell, okay, I'm on my way. Stay calm, mate, you're the first on scene and you have to cope. Make sure everyone's breathing—concentrate on getting muck away from their mouths and noses, and make sure no one's slumped so they're restricting their air flow. I'll be with you in minutes. Go.'

His phone was back in his pocket and he hauled the door open.

She knew what she'd heard. A car crash. Multiple casualties.

'Do you need help?' she demanded.

'No,' he snapped.

He strode two steps out the door, and then stopped. Took a grip. Saw sense.

'Yes,' he said, without looking back. 'There's been a head-on collision two miles on the other side of town, just past my place. That was a local farmer. Four injuries, and from the sound of it they're bad. The ambulance is fifty miles away. Yes, I might need help. I'd appreciate it if you came.'

CHAPTER TWELVE

HE SHOULDN'T focus on anything but the task ahead. But after a fast call to the police and to the ambulance service, with two miles between them and the crash site there was room for more.

Erin was staring straight ahead. He'd hurt her, he thought. He'd watched as her features had flattened, from eager, laughing, even maybe seductive, to humiliation and anger.

Her impulse to stay here, made in hours, was nuts.

She was just like his mother.

The thought slammed home and it hurt. He only vaguely remembered his mother, but what he remembered was flatness and apathy. Except for the times she'd arrived home 'in love'.

'Oh, Dom, this is wonderful, this is different, this will totally transform our lives.'

And it always did. The fragile security they achieved in between his mother's romantic attachments—a place to call home, school routine, belongings—was cast to the wind as they followed one loser after another.

Even at seven he'd remembered saying desperately to his mother, 'How can you be in love after only one night? How can you decide to move without even thinking about it?'

He glanced across at Erin and saw that was exactly where she was. She was all for throwing the old life away and starting the new, just because it was exciting, different and wonderful.

It wasn't wonderful, he told himself grimly. She'd wake up and realise what was important—Charles, her parents, her career. And he'd be responsible.

'You always mess things up for me.' Hell, where had that come from? His mother's voice, sobbing from the past. *'He'd want me if I didn't have you. Don't whine, Dominic, we'll find somewhere else to live and next time be smarter. Just stay in the background. I don't know…disappear.'*

He had. He'd ended up in foster-care—thank God, with Ruby—and his mother had never come back for him.

Impulsive decisions were for fools. Relationships sucked. Love at first sight was for idiots.

He glanced across at Erin and he felt his gut clench. He had no intention of making her miserable. But the way he felt about her…

He might even imagine himself in love with her. But if he did…if he stayed round her for much longer…it'd just make everything worse.

The accident was about half a mile past Dom's home. They passed his house, going at speed. Erin glanced fleetingly at the driveway and Charles's car was still parked in front.

'Call him,' Dom said before she could say anything. 'Frank said we have multiple casualties. If Charles is another doctor and he's prepared to help…'

'You must really be desperate,' Erin muttered, but she used her cellphone and waited for Charles to answer.

Charles's phone rang through to the message bank. Odd. And what was he doing, still there?

It couldn't matter. Dom had rounded the last bend and the crash was in view.

It looked shocking. Horrific.

A purple kombi van was on the wrong side of the road. It looked as if it had hit a sedan, then spun, so the sedan had smashed full on into the kombi's side.

The sedan was a crumpled mess. The trunk had torn open. Baggage had been thrown out onto the road. A child's doll was lying on the verge, looking like a small, dreadful corpse.

A guy in khaki overalls and boots bigger than Erin's was holding a little girl in his arms. The child was sobbing uncontrollably, screaming for her mother.

'That's Frank, the farmer who called us,' Dom said. 'Hell, we'll need some local help as well. Ring Graham.'

He hit the brakes and was out of the car, clicking onto a number and tossing her his phone before Erin could respond.

Okay. First things first, follow orders, but there was no way she was calmly sitting in the car making phone calls. She was out of the car as well, running toward the wreck as Dom hauled gear out of the trunk.

'Car smash, two miles out of town past Dom's place,' she snapped as Graham answered. 'Dom and I are here. We've called the ambulance but we need more help.'

'I'll have the boys there in minutes,' Graham said, and Erin thought fleetingly, The man's been up all night and here he was, helping out again. Local communities at their best. But then she stopped thinking. She was at the wreck now, and what she saw…

It was a family sedan. The van was higher than the sedan and the front of the sedan was wedged right under the van's chassis.

Dom was already working. They only had access on the left side. The door of the car had been hauled open. Dom was half in, working on whoever was closest.

'I got the little girl out 'cos she was screaming,' Frank called hopelessly from behind them. 'I don't know what—'

'Just take care of her,' Dom called. 'It's okay. We'll deal with this.'

It wasn't okay.

The woman closest to them was in her thirties or early forties. She was staring straight ahead, whimpering in shock and fear.

'Sharon, hey, it's okay, let's get you out,' Dom said and she turned her face a little.

'D-Dom.'

So Dom knew them. That made it…worse.

A vicious gash ran down the side of Sharon's head from just above her ear. She had the look of someone just returning from unconsciousness, Erin thought. Dom was mopping blood from around her mouth. Erin reached through from the front and took her wrist. Her pulse was thready and her complexion was sickly blue.

'Does it hurt to breathe?' Dom asked.

'N-No.'

They had to get her out to reach her partner. There was another child in the back seat.

So much blood. Far too much blood.

Erin wriggled in underneath Dom and slid her hands across the seat, feeling for any obstructions.

'My hands are under her knees,' Erin said curtly. 'Seat belt undone?'

'Yes.'

'On count of three, lift.'

They lifted. Blessedly she came free.

They worked as if they'd been trained together. Dom must have done the same emergency training she'd done, Erin thought appreciatively. They had Sharon away from the wreck in seconds, carrying her over to the verge to where Frank still stood helplessly holding the child.

They laid her on the grass. Erin had been doing a lightning assessment as they'd moved her. The moment they had her down Dom was moving back to the wreck. Erin gave Sharon a moment more, checking vital signs.

Her airway was clear. The gash on her head was bleeding but not gushing. They had her on her side so the blood was no longer running down her face.

There were fractures, she thought, glancing at the woman's leg, but she was breathing steadily and was conscious.

There was no time to check for more.

'Stay with her,' she said to Frank. 'Sit down beside her with the little girl.' She took Sharon's hand. 'Sharon, Dom and I need to get everyone else out of the car. Frank will look after you and your daughter.'

It was all she had time for. She was away, back to Dom.

Dom had the little boy out of the car before she reached him. One look at him and she knew there was urgent need, but Dom was tugging the little boy past her.

'See to his dad,' he snapped to her. 'I have Max. His dad's name is Ivan and he's in trouble.'

So was the little boy. The child's face was a mass of blood but Dom's command had been urgent and unequivocal.

Ivan, the boy's father, was crumpled against the far side of the car. The steering-wheel was crushed against his chest. Even from here she could see the effort it was for him to breathe. His breathing came as short sharp gasps. His hand was on his chest, and he looked frantic.

Triage.

'No,' she said, pulling back in fast decision. Ivan had to be pulled from the car before she could help him and it couldn't be a lift. Because of the urgency it would have to be a messy pull, and she couldn't do it. She lifted Max from Dom's arms without waiting for him to respond. 'Ivan can't breathe and he needs your strength. Get him out of there. I'll take over with Max. Breathing tubes?'

'In the case.'

'Thank God for that.'

The little boy's breath was bubbling as if he was breathing underwater. Something had smashed into his face. With the amount of blood in his mouth and nose, he was likely to drown.

Moving fast, she laid him on the verge, close to his mother. His nose was broken, there were smashed teeth—the little boy would need reconstructive surgery. But that was for the future. For now all she could do was clear his mouth and throat, set him on his side, fit an oral airway and administer oxygen. Thank God for Dom's equipment.

Thank God for Dom.

The little boy had gone past terror. He hadn't enough strength left to fight her; he simply submitted.

'You'll be safe, Max,' she told him. 'You can breathe now, and I'm giving you something to stop it hurting. I'm popping a mask over your face to make it easier to breathe.' She manoeuvred him so he was lying propped against his mother. Frank was still holding the little girl, looking more and more terrified by the minute.

Where on earth was help?

'Can you set the little girl down on the grass?' she said to Frank, and then to Sharon, 'Can you please hold your daughter's hand? I need Frank to hold Max's mask in place.' Then, as no one moved, she lifted the little girl bodily from Frank's grasp and set her down by her mother. Then she grabbed Frank's big, weather-beaten hands, tugged him down so he was forced to crouch, and forcibly put his hand over Max's mask.

'Hold that,' she ordered. 'Don't any of you move. Frank, if that mask moves…if Max looks like he's not getting enough air, if there's anything that scares you, then you yell loud enough to wake the dead and I'll be back. But Dom needs me.'

Dom did need her.

He had Ivan out of the car but Ivan's breathing was so shallow it was barely there.

Erin took a moment to watch as Dom worked. Ivan's chest was hardly moving—one side seemed totally still. Dom's fingers were on his throat and he sent her a silent message with his eyes. She knew what it had to be. He'd have felt Ivan's trachea, and found it pushed to one side.

This had to be a tension pneumothorax. The symptoms fitted. He'd have broken ribs and a puncture to his lung, so air was escaping from his lung into his chest every time he breathed. The air couldn't be exhaled. The pressure would be enough to collapse both lungs.

Dominic had obviously already made the diagnosis. He was grabbing what he needed from his bag. He had a cannula between his teeth, still in its protective sterile casing, holding it while he ripped the side of Ivan's shirt from neck to waist.

She grabbed a sterile swab from the bag. Dom looked like he'd been going in without—there was no time for niceties here when the only imperative was to save the man's life. But she moved like lightning, hauling the swab open, swabbing Ivan's chest, noting the enlarged veins in his neck, how the left side of his chest wasn't responding even when he managed to take a breath.

Air would be being sucked out into the chest wall, building, building, so the lungs could no longer expand, so no more air could get in. He was hardly breathing at all, just sharp, tiny gasps that did nothing to alleviate the blue of his lips and the terror in his eyes.

They had to get the pressure off.

She pulled her hand away, leaving the path clear for Dom— but suddenly the cannula was in her hand.

'You're the emergency specialist,' Dom snapped. 'You go in.'

She didn't argue. At one level she appreciated Dom's hard-headedness. That morning he'd objected when she'd taken over his patient—and so he should. But now he was deferring to her specialist training, ego aside.

He was already moving on, fitting an oxygen mask, leaving her to what she had to do.

She positioned the needle with care but with speed, then pushed in with force. Deep within the chest.

Over the top of the sixth rib, in line with the axilla, into the thoracic cavity.

The air hissed out like a burst of steam under pressure.

She'd done this once before and then it had been too late. Please…

It wasn't too late now. Ivan's next breaths, miraculously, were slower, and his chest rose and fell. Rose and fell.

They'd done it.

Dom had fitted an oxygen mask over Ivan's face. The man's colour was improving already.

Blessed be Dom's medical kit, Erin thought again, thankfully. He had four oxygen cylinders. Four!

'You'll have to restock oxygen before your football team goes diving again,' she whispered, allowing herself a tiny release from tension as Ivan took another breath that actually worked, letting air into his chest and making his chest wall rise and fall almost normally.

They needed to get him to hospital, fast. He needed a chest tube and an underwater seal fitted until his lung had a chance to heal, but with the pressure off, the other lung could work and he should survive.

And they were no longer alone. There were suddenly vehicles everywhere. The cavalry had arrived—in force.

'Hey,' Dom said in a voice that was suddenly a bit unsteady. His hand was on Ivan's shoulder. His words might be for him but he was looking at Erin. 'We've done it. Well done. Ivan, you're going to be okay, mate. We've sucked a ruddy great air pocket out of your chest. Or rather Doc Erin has. We're bloody lucky to have her.'

And then, as Erin's eyes filled unaccountably with tears, he went on to answer the unspoken questions in Ivan's eyes. 'Sharon and the kids are going to be okay. You're going to be okay.'

Erin left him to it. She stumbled—her legs unaccountably weren't working properly—over to the verge to do the same thing for Sharon.

'Your husband and your kids will live.'

It could have been so much worse.

'Where's the driver of the kombi?' someone demanded.

It was Graham—of course. He was wearing—of all things—a kilt. Later she'd discover that the local Highland band had been practicing. Everyone round them was wearing kilts. Her sense of unreality deepened. A nightmare, with kilts.

'I couldn't find him,' Frank said. The farmer was still seated on the verge, one arm full of the little girl, the other holding the little boy's mask in place. Erin put a hand on the little girl's neck and felt her pulse. It was strong and steady.

'I reckon she's gone to sleep, Doc,' Frank said, and Erin smiled—her first real smile for the evening. She left the little girl and turned her attention to Sharon's leg. This would heal, she thought.

But Dom wasn't relaxing. He was staring around, focusing on Graham's question. 'The kombi driver... Where the hell...?'

'He wasn't here when I got here, Doc,' Frank said. 'Swear to God. I heard the smash from the dairy. I was only a couple of minutes away but he was gone.'

The cab of the kombi was almost intact. Empty. Had he been thrown? Or...

'I need to go,' Dom said, urgently, as the scream of an approaching ambulance cut the night. 'Erin, can you take over here? They'll all have to be taken to Campbelltown or air ambulanced to Melbourne. I'll leave that call to you. But everyone's stablised.'

'What's wrong?'

He closed his eyes, briefly. She reached instinctively for his hand and he held it, hard. Only for a fraction of a second, though, as if needing strength before moving on.

'I think this is Nathan's dad's van,' he told her. 'I have to go.'

There were two ambulances. The paramedics were competent officers accustomed to dealing with emergencies a long way from the city. Dom and Erin had done the hard stuff. They moved in, setting up drips, stemming bleeding, moving parents and children into the two vehicles, making sure they were stabilised.

Erin helped transfer them but they didn't need her to go with them. She watched them leave, feeling ill, shattered at how fast an evening drive could come so close to tragedy. But…where was Dom?

'Is there any sign the driver of the kombi was hurt?' she asked, and Graham shook his head.

'We don't think so. The cab's intact and there's no blood, nor is there any sign he's been thrown clear. It doesn't tell you for sure he wasn't hurt but…' He shrugged. 'No matter. The police will find him.'

Her concern grew. She had time now to stop and think through Dom's reaction when he'd realised who the driver of the kombi was. She'd been caught up, focusing on Sharon's leg when Dom had told her. Now she replayed his words—and remembered fear.

Why?

The man was a drug addict. Unpredictable. Unstable.

Nathan was afraid of him.

Unbidden, Dom's words came back to her. 'I take kids where there's a problem—a reason they need closer supervision than foster-parents can give.'

Problems like Martin's mother, intent on harm. Nathan's father, arriving on Friday looking ready to do violence. Back here today. Why?

She stood and surveyed the whole crash scene in its entirety.

'What do you reckon happened?' she asked Graham, who looked like he was doing the same thing.

'The cops have been looking at the tyre marks,' Graham said. 'It looks like the kombi driver was on the wrong side of the road. The cops are saying he didn't even swerve. Ivan did all the work, trying to avoid him.'

'Then the driver of the kombi…' Her breath caught in fear. 'Graham, can we leave others to finish here? I need to go back to Dom's.'

* * *

She outlined her fears to Graham on the short drive, hoping she sounded worried for no reason, but Graham's face confirmed what she was thinking.

'He and Tansy take on the kids no one else will have,' he said grimly. 'Kids who'd otherwise go into juvenile detention, just to get the protection they need. But Dom can talk down the worst of them. I've seen him with a hopheaded father out of his brain with drugs and Dom just talked and talked, getting more and more boring till the guy's eyes glazed over and the threat was past. Tansy, too.'

'Tansy's boring?'

'She's a ball-breaker,' Graham said, and grinned. 'I'd like to see any hophead get past our Tansy.'

It made her feel better—but not much. 'Can we hurry?'

'We're already there,' Graham said.

She was no longer listening. The moment the car stopped she was out, running toward the house, stumbling slightly in her stupid boots but still running.

He'd been there.

The front door was open. There was a hole smashed in the panelling. Splintered timber.

There were voices coming from the kitchen. Dom. Charles.

She bucketed through.

Tansy was sitting in front of the fire. There was blood spattered down the front of her gorgeous shawl. Charles was bathing her forehead, an expression on his face she'd never seen before.

Ruby was sitting on the opposite side of the fire. She had Martin on her knees, rocking him like a baby. 'It's okay,' she was crooning. 'He's gone. You saw the police take him away. We'll find Nathan.'

Dom was standing with his back to the door, barking orders into his phone. As Erin entered he wheeled to face her. 'Erin,' he said blankly and then, as he saw Graham behind her, he said, 'Graham, thank God. I've been trying to reach you.'

'I dropped the phone on the road back at the crash,' Graham said briskly. 'Smashed. What's up?'

'I need help.' He stared blankly at both of them and she couldn't help it. Erin crossed the few steps separating them, she put her hands in his and held.

Her Dom. He was, she thought. This man's trouble was her trouble, whether he willed it or not.

'What's happened?'

'He came here,' he said. 'Nathan's dad. Off his head with drugs. He'd heard about the fire—hell, there's been no news over Easter so the local radio station played it as a major event. He must have crashed but he still came. He said his son wasn't safe and he was taking him away. When Nathan said he didn't want to go, he hit him. Tansy intervened and got hit herself.'

'Oh, Tansy…'

'But Charles helped,' Tansy whispered. 'Nathan broke free. He headed across the road into bushland. Charles managed to stop Michael going after him. A couple of cops on the way to the accident stopped and lent a hand. They've arrested Michael and taken him away, but Nathan's disappeared. He just ran straight into the bush.'

'I've been into the bush as far as I dare,' Dom said grimly. 'I've yelled my lungs out.' He turned to Graham, his face set and hard. 'I need you mate,' he told him. 'I need everyone. I want him found.'

CHAPTER THIRTEEN

THIS town was amazing. These people were amazing. The more Erin saw of them the more she wanted to be a part of this community.

Last night half the town had been up to a fire. Now they were turning out to search for one little boy.

She wasn't allowed to help.

'Your feet...you shouldn't be walking on them at all, much less traipsing round the countryside looking for Nathan,' Dom growled.

Search parties seemed to be organising themselves, men and women dividing the district into grids, acting methodically and fast. Dom was desperate to be gone as well—he organised himself to lead the first search party but Graham wanted him close. He had to physically hold him back while he made him see sense.

'So we find him,' Graham told him. 'Or we think we know where he is. The kid's terrified. You need to be on call to go wherever we need, to stop him running.'

'I can do that,' Tansy ventured.

'You can't.' It was Charles, and once again Erin had that flash of something she hadn't seen from Charles.

Charles had known Tansy for, what, four hours? Was there something in the water?

'He knocked you out,' Charles was saying. 'You're not doing anything until we get that head X-rayed.'

'I can do the calling,' Ruby said diffidently, but Dom shook his head. Grim but accepting.

'No. Graham's right,' Dom said. 'And so's Charles. I'll stay. Tansy needs an X-ray—if there's a fracture and we miss it I'd never forgive myself and I want it done by someone more capable of reading results than me. Cracked ribs are one thing—neurology's another. Can you take her to Campbelltown, Charles?'

'Sure.'

'And Martin and I will keep the home fires burning,' Ruby said. It was a platitude, said so serenely that it sounded right, and Erin saw in that moment why Dom was so grateful for Ruby's care that he'd taken on fostering himself. She saw Dom nod and knew that somehow he'd been unaccountably comforted by this elderly little woman with her prosaic attitude to life.

Strangely, inexplicably it hurt. She wanted to do the comforting. If he'd only let her.

But… 'Can you get one of the guys to drop Erin at her place?' Dom asked Graham.

'No!' she said, startled.

'Yes,' he said, and suddenly Dom's voice was steely. 'You're injured and I will not drag you into our lives even further.'

'I don't think she needs to be dragged,' Ruby said placidly.

'No matter,' Dom said, still harsh. He met her gaze full on. 'Erin, I can't afford to be distracted. It causes… It's caused… No. Just go. Please.'

It was hard to get her voice to work. They were all looking at her. She knew her distress was showing but she didn't care. Dom's expression was implacable. He really didn't want her.

'You'll…you'll let me know when you find him?' she whispered.

'Of course we will,' Ruby said warmly but Dom had already turned away to talk to Graham.

* * *

So she went home. One of the searchers drove her—they were starting their search in the town and working their way back through the bush.

She was dropped off at her new home. It was growing dark. And cold. Or maybe that was just her.

She let herself into the house and Marilyn greeted her with joy. She knelt, she hugged her dog—and she burst into tears.

'What will I do, Marilyn?' she sobbed. 'I love him to distraction. I love them all to distraction.'

In response the dog gave her a huge dog-kiss, from chin to nose. Erin hiccuped on a sob, it turned into a sort of laugh and she tried to haul herself together.

'We'll be okay,' she whispered. 'You and me. We'll be fine. Oh, but Nathan…and Dom…'

Dom would be going out of his mind, pacing, waiting for news. She ought to be there.

He wouldn't let her.

'How he expects me to calmly go to bed,' she said savagely to Marilyn. 'I can't. Okay, my feet hurt, but they're getting better. Socks and trainers would support them so they don't hurt. I could search.

'But you don't know the area,' she admitted to herself. She didn't feel like she had any common sense left, but what there was surfaced for a moment. 'You don't know where to look. Your feet are sore and you'd hold searchers back. Or you'd get yourself lost.'

Lost. The word itself was frightening. The area around the town was thick bushland. If Nathan was hiding…

It was wild.

'I wouldn't go into the bush if I was Nathan,' she told Marilyn, and Marilyn wagged her butt in agreement.

'Neither would you,' Erin said, hugging her tight for she had to hug someone. 'Where would I go if I was Nathan?'

That was easy. 'I'd go find Dom. Me and Nathan both,' she said to Marilyn, giving her a shame-faced grin. 'I have it bad.'

So if Nathan was looking for Dom…

'He'd go out to the car crash,' she decided. Really, this was quite a sensible conversation. Erin v. Erin.

'No, he wouldn't,' she said. 'He'd think Dom was here.' She was thinking it through and relaying her thoughts to Marilyn. 'This afternoon Dom left home to bring me here. As far as Nathan knows, Dom is still here. I bet he knows where this place is. And it's…'

She paused. Lightbulb moment. 'It's about three miles from Dom's place, just around the headland,' she breathed. 'Nathan thinks his father is looking for him. Would he go by road?

'I wouldn't,' she told Marilyn, answering herself. 'I'd go by the beach. I couldn't get lost that way. I'd get out of sight of the house and then I'd sneak back over to the beach. I could hide under the cliffs and I'd think no one would look for me there.'

So, ring Dom and tell him.

She lifted her phone from her pocket and paused.

They'd already have thought of it, she decided. And the way Dom had looked at her…like she'd distracted him and this was the result…

He didn't need any more distraction.

And she didn't actually know his phone number.

But…

But.

'You reckon the puppies can do without you for a few minutes?' she asked Marilyn. 'I know this is a big ask, but it's dark on the beach and I wouldn't mind company.'

Dom was going nuts, pacing in the darkness, waiting for news. More than anything else, he wanted to join the searchers, to yell his lungs out as half the town was doing. But Graham was right. He had to be accessible if Nathan needed to be coaxed out of hiding.

The country west of the road was wild and mountainous. A little boy would lose himself quickly.

And stay lost?

The thought didn't bear thinking, but it was with him and it wouldn't go.

Nathan had been gone for two hours. Terrified, he could have travelled fast.

I'll be crossed off the list of foster-parents after this, he thought grimly. Even if Nathan was found. He'd had to do a hard sell to be allowed to take these two boys. Both, it had been argued, would be safer in a secure facility.

And suddenly he thought, I wouldn't mind keeping them.

The thought was like a sunbeam piercing through thick cloud. To keep these boys… To give emotional commitment, long term…

He'd been walking back and forth along the headland behind the house, watching the moonlit beach, desperate to see a small figure struggling home. But the tide was almost full. Nathan would have to be off the beach. There was nowhere to hide there.

The thought wasn't fading. He wouldn't mind keeping them.

Martin and Nathan.

He'd had Martin for six months now, and Nathan for only a little less. It was the longest he'd ever had kids.

They were great little boys, brimful of potential. Scarred by life, they were starting to emerge from that scarring and become great.

Every other child he'd cared for he'd said goodbye to with a sense of relief. His plan—what he did for all of them—was to care for them while there was a threat, then pass them on. Tansy did the warm and fuzzy stuff. She'd divorced early from a bad marriage. She loved the kids. He provided the house, the security. She did the rest.

But now…

He wanted more.

And he wanted Erin.

After two days?

Stupid.

Only maybe it wasn't stupid. What if such a thing really existed? His mother had believed in it with her whole heart. Love at first sight.

What if Erin was…it?

She was messing with his head. Erin. Nathan. Erin.

Martin. Marilyn.

Erin.

His…family?

Okay, so she'd just walk slowly along the beach. Carefully, so her feet didn't hurt. She wasn't holding anyone up and she couldn't get lost. She was her own personal little search party.

Marilyn strolled a couple of hundred yards with her, then looked apologetically up at her. I have my pups, her look said. But I'd rather be doing what you're doing.

She turned and headed sedately back along the beach.

So it was dark and she was alone, with just a torch for company. She couldn't go much further, anyway. Half a mile from her house the headland became rocky and hard to negotiate. She'd found the torch in the kitchen cupboard but she didn't know how long the battery would last. The last thing she wanted was to become another person on the lost list.

Okay, she conceded finally. Dom was right. Her feet hurt. And she'd run out of beach. The cliffs loomed dark and dangerous. There was no way Nathan could get round here at high tide.

But a little voice was still whispering. If he'd tried and the tide had come in…

She should go home.

But first…

Crazy or not, she picked her way over the rocks, as far as she could before it got downright dangerous. Then she stared out into the night, waiting for there to be a pause in the crash of the surf.

Waiting.

Then, 'Nathan!' She yelled it with all the power she could muster.

She ached to hear. She wanted to hear so much that when she did she thought she was imagining it.

But no. It was a child's thin voice, high and terrified.

'Help me.'

Dammit, he'd ring her.

He'd rung every set of searchers. He'd paced so long he was practically paced out. He was going crazy.

Nathan. Nathan.

And along with it, like an echo, Erin. Erin.

Erin couldn't help. But he could just...phone. He had her number to let her know when Nathan was found.

It wasn't a real weakness. It wasn't like he was admitting he needed her. He was just giving her an update.

Four rings. Five.

It switched to the message bank.

The phone would be inside and she'd be outside, pacing. He knew it as surely as he knew himself.

He knew her. And he'd hurt her.

She'd offered to be with him and he'd knocked her back— but it was more than offering to be with him. That was why he'd sent her away. They both knew what was happening between them.

Hell, his head was doing him in. He wanted Nathan to be found so he could concentrate on something else.

Like Erin.

'She seems lovely.' It was Ruby, coming up behind him.

He groaned.

'Nathan'll be safe,' Ruby said with quiet confidence. 'You kids used to run away all the time. The townspeople won't give up till they find him.' She tucked her arm into his. 'You have a whole community of caring. Not bad for a loner.'

'I'm not.'

'A loner?' She put her wrinkled hand into his and held hard. 'I know. As I said, she seems lovely.'

'Ruby, it's way too soon. I've known her for less than three days.'

'It's never too soon,' she said serenely. 'You've been waiting all your life for this. Don't be ridiculous.'

'She's not answering her phone.'

She picked her way gingerly over the rocky outcrop. The cliff face was sheer, but part of the cliff had caved in years before to form a sort of path between cliff and sea.

She climbed maybe two hundred yards, her torch playing out ahead, trying to see where the cry had come from.

Once she slipped. She fell, only a couple of feet but it scared her. She clambered back, vaguely aware her phone was ringing.

Nathan was screaming again and she forgot about her phone. For now it wasn't a come-and-get-me scream. It was a scream of sheer terror. From the sea.

She steadied and shone her torch across the waves.

He was maybe twenty feet from the base of the cliff, forty or fifty yards from her, on what was a tiny rocky island. He must have been trying to reach the ledge where she was when the tide had beaten him.

The tide was still rising. While she watched, another wave smashed over his tiny island.

He was down on all fours, screaming and clinging. Erin sucked in her breath in horror. She had to wait for the wave to recede to see if he was still there.

He was—but only just. Once more wave would push him in.

Some things were just plain dumb. Like jumping into the sea, in the dark as the wind was rising.

But the wave was receding, giving her a moment's calm. It was all the time she had—and she was all Nathan had.

She slid from her ledge and struck out for Nathan.

* * *

'So why isn't she answering the phone?'

'I don't know, dear,' Ruby said. 'Maybe she isn't carrying it. Some people have been known to live to a ripe old age without ever owning a cellphone.'

He smiled but his smile was perfunctory. 'The first time I rang, it rang out. Now it says the phone's turned off or out of range. There's no way she'll have turned it off. She's as worried as I am.'

'Yet you sent her home.'

'Okay. I'm a fool. But now…'

'It's probably out of battery,' Ruby said wisely. 'You young ones spend your lives looking for phone chargers or getting cross 'cos your battery's flat.'

'We recharged her battery last night.'

'Maybe it got soot in it.' She regarded him sideways. 'You know what? You're going to have to find out.'

'I can't leave here. You heard Graham.'

'I heard Graham tell us you need to be available if any of the search parties need you. I suspect Erin's made up her own search party. I suspect she needs you.'

'You think?'

'Hey, don't ask me,' Ruby said wryly. 'I'm just an old lady who doesn't own a cellphone. But I'm here and I can talk Nathan out of a hidey-hole at a hundred paces if need be. Martin's asleep. I can go to Nathan if they need me. So you go look for Nathan yourself. Look for Erin, too.' She smiled and reached up to kiss him on the cheek. 'And while you're about it, what about searching for your family at the same time?'

Nathan's 'island' was eight feet wide at its widest. In the centre was a jagged knob. That's why he hadn't been swept off—he'd been able to cling to it.

Erin swam the few yards to the rock in record time. She hauled herself up onto the ledge then grabbed Nathan and the rocky knob as another breaker crashed over them.

It took all her strength to hold on. When the wave receded, Nathan was stuck to her like a limpet, holding on with hands and feet, and she was clutching the knob beyond him.

With the incoming tide this was only going to get worse. It was a miracle Nathan had held on this long.

'Can you swim?'

'N-no.'

'Then you'll have to float,' she said, spitting water. 'And let me hold you. But, Nathan, if you try and hold me, we'll both drown.'

'I'm scared.'

'Me, too.' So much for reassurance, but it seemed to work. Nathan seemed to steady. The bravery of him... All of five years old and he was a hero.

A smaller wave washed over them. They didn't go under this time but another wave was bearing down.

'After this next one,' Erin said, urgently. 'We'll roll back into the water and let the wave push us toward the cliff. As soon as the wave's past you lie on your back and I'll tow you. If another wave comes you're not to panic—just hold your nose and wait till it passes. I'll hold you around your shoulders. You're not to try and grab me 'cos I have to use all my energy to swim. Do you think you can do that?'

'Is Dom coming?' Nathan quavered.

'Of course he is,' Erin said. 'Here's the wave, Nathe. Ready, set, go.'

She wasn't at the house but Marilyn was in the kitchen, pacing back and forth to the back door.

'So where's your mistress?' Dom said, crouching down and fondling her ears. 'What have you done with her?'

As if in answer, Marilyn crossed to the open back door and stared anxiously into the night.

Toward the beach.

'I told her not to search,' Dom said, so savagely that Marilyn looked up at him in surprise. He relented and crouched down to give her another pat. 'I s'pose you think that's dumb. Telling Erin to keep out of my life.'

Marilyn groaned in agreement—or maybe because she really liked what Dom was doing behind her ears.

But doggy massage wasn't on the agenda. 'Okay,' he said, and straightened. 'Let's assume she's gone along the beach. I'm guessing she's heading toward my place.'

He should wait for help. For back-up. But…

'Everyone's looking for Nathan,' he told Marilyn. 'I don't want them to stop just because one dumb, female doctor…'

Who you happen to love…

Where had that come from? No matter—it just had—and once thought couldn't be retracted.

'Okay, who I just happen to love,' he said, resigned. 'Regardless. She's risking her neck and her feet walking along the beach at high tide in the dark. But who am I to query her motives? Okay, Marilyn, while we wait for the rest of the world to find Nathan, I need to find Erin.'

She had Nathan safe. For now. She was shoving him out of the water onto the rock ledge she'd set off from, but even as she did so she saw their escape route had been cut off.

Part of the ledge she'd clambered over was now awash.

At least the rocks they were on now were dry. She hauled herself up after Nathan, she hugged him tight and she tried to assess whether they could clamber back to the beach between waves.

The answer was no. The sea was building; the strengthening wind whipping up waves already swelling with the tide. It had been risky enough trying to get Nathan here. She daren't move any further.

At least the rock they were on wasn't slippery. Maybe it was higher than the high-water mark.

Please…

'Will Dom come and find us?' Nathan asked in a tiny voice, and she hugged him close and thought he was such a brave little kid. Brave beyond his years. To be allocated a father like Michael…

It wasn't fair. She wanted…she wanted…

She knew what she wanted. Dom only took kids in peril. When the peril was past…if she could manoeuvre her way round the challenge of Nathan's appalling father…if Dom didn't want Nathan…if Dom didn't want her…

'I seem to be adding to my family,' she told Nathan, hugging him close. 'Me and Marilyn and three puppies. And now you, if I can find a way to wiggle you into my life. If we can figure what to do with your dad. They say the heart expands to fit all comers. I wonder how my mum and dad feel about becoming grandparents?'

'Erin!' Dom was shouting into the rising wind, starting to worry in earnest as he saw the sea building. Storms could arrive without warning, and this had all the signs of being a beauty.

Dear God, Nathan was out in it. And Erin…

What the hell was she playing at? 'Erin!'

'Cooee.'

He stopped dead.

'Erin?'

'Cooee.' It was the Australian bush call, echoing over the waves. Where…?

There was no way she could have got further than the ledge he'd reached. Where…?

'Cooee?'

She must have reached further. Before the tide came in?

Dammit, was she trying to kill herself? Didn't she know—?

'Cooee.'

'Alright, I'm coming,' he said grimly. 'Hold on.'

Their ledge was precarious. It might be safe for a little longer but the waves were already reaching just beneath the rock they were on.

Swimming out to Nathan, the sea had at least been clear. Here, though, the partial cliff collapse meant the sea was churning round jagged rocks. On her own she might have clambered back, knowing she'd probably be able to haul herself out if she was washed in. With Nathan, though…not.

He'd been extraordinarily brave. He'd lain limply in her grasp as she'd towed him here, and for a five-year-old to do that…

She was so proud of him she could cry, but she couldn't take him further. Neither could she leave him to get help.

Her phone was dead—salt water wasn't great for reception. All they could do was wait. And hope.

'He'll come, won't he?' Nathan asked again, through chattering teeth.

'Of course he will,' Erin said, but it sounded hollow even to her.

Stay or go? Damned if she did, damned if she didn't.

Stay. There was no choice.

She held onto Nathan, she hugged him and she prayed. Dom, Dom, Dom.

'Erin…'

When had her name ever sounded as good?

'Cooee.'

She'd expected him to go for help. She'd never thought he'd clamber round the rocks.

He was ten yards away before she saw him in the moonlight. He'd been washed from a rock and had a handhold again, hauling himself out of the sea and up to safety.

She didn't move. Nathan was hugged hard against her and it was Nathan who was directing traffic.

'We're up here. Dom, look out, there's another wave, duck, hurry, we're here.'

He'd reach them, she thought, mistily. Her kelpie. *'I am a man upon the land, I am a kelpie upon the sea…'*

She sang it with joy in her heart. Nathan stared at her like she'd lost her mind, and Dom hauled himself up the last rock and heard what she was singing. He stared at her as if he couldn't believe his eyes—and then he burst out laughing.

He gathered the pair of them into his arms.

And then he kissed her.

CHAPTER FOURTEEN

FIRST things first. Or, rather, second, because the kiss came first but that didn't count as it was imperative. Erin tugged herself from Dom's hold and smiled mistily at her love.

'I knew you'd come.'

'Marilyn told me you were here.'

'Good old Marilyn,' she said happily. 'I rescued her and she's rescued me right back. But, Dom…'

'Mmm?' He held her tight, with Nathan squeezed somewhere in between.

'I dare say you didn't think about it on your very noble climb around here but we can't climb back and my phone got wet. The tide's still coming in. These waves are getting higher. And if I'm not mistaken, your phone just got wet too.'

'Yeah, but I phoned before I climbed,' he said lovingly, and she blinked.

'You phoned?'

'Triage,' he said. 'What they taught us in medical school. Think about danger—i.e. personal safety first.'

'You're wonderful,' she said happily. There was no earthly reason to be happy. She was soaked, she was battered, she wasn't in the least bit safe—yet—and here she was, grinning like a fool just because this man had put himself in the same deadly peril she was in.

'I love you,' he said, and she stopped grinning.

'P-pardon?'

'I think you heard,' Dom said. He hauled Nathan onto his knee. Dom was sitting on the end of their ledge, his feet hanging over the side so his already soaking feet got even wetter. It didn't look like he cared, though. 'Do you think she heard, Nathe?'

'You said you loved her,' Nathan said. 'Why?'

'Good question,' Dom said.

'Um…Dom?'

'Yes, my love,' he said, so lovingly she thought she'd drowned and gone to heaven. But this wouldn't do, she told herself severely, trying to focus on something other than what he'd just said. There was a certain amount of triage she needed to do herself if this wasn't to be the shortest engagement in the history of the world.

'Um…you said you rang before you came.'

'I did,' he said—modestly. 'I told Graham I thought you were stuck on a cliff at Moonlight Bluff—that's where we're sitting, by the way. I said if he didn't hear back within ten minutes could he contact the authorities and get a helicopter.'

'You didn't,' she breathed.

'I know—Mr Wonderful,' he said modestly, and she choked.

'Um…how do we know the helicopter's free to come save us?' she asked. She shouldn't ask. Nathan had relaxed, slumping against Dom, feeling safe and loved and…home. Like she wanted to be. And she could be, she thought, dazed. She just had to get these niggling worries sorted first. Like whether or not they were going to drown.

'We don't,' Dom said. 'So I've organised one of the fishermen to bring his boat round from the harbour and play floodlights on the cliff.' He peered out into the darkness. 'He ought to be here any minute. If the helicopter doesn't arrive, Graham's organising guys to abseil from the cliff top and haul us up.' He winced as a wave splashed to his thighs. 'I hope they hurry. You guys have got the best spot. I'm getting cold.'

'You didn't order a heater and hot soup while you were at it, I suppose,' she said waspishly, and he grinned.

'Didn't think of it,' he admitted. 'Now—where were we? Oh, yes. I love you.'

'Seriously...'

'Seriously,' he said, and suddenly his tone *was* serious. 'I know. Love at first sight is impossible. At least, that's what I thought. I can't believe it's taken me three days to admit I'm wrong. But I felt it the moment I saw you. I wanted you. Then I thought it's crazy. All the time you were helping me, even offering to work here, I was thinking this was nuts, I must be nuts. What do they say? Marry in haste, repent at leisure? That's what I believed. And then...the car crash...' Another wave hit his legs. 'Wow, this water's cold.'

'Don't you dare stop,' she said. 'I don't care how cold the water is. This is a story I need to hear right through to the end.'

'Okay.' His voice gentled and his hand gripped hers. 'Okay, I stood at the car crash and I saw how close that little family had come to being wiped out. And you know what I thought? I thought at least they'd had each other. They were with each other. And I thought, even if I died right now—which, mind you, if this water gets any colder is on the cards...'

'Shut up and talk,' she said lovingly.

'Yeah, well,' he said, and sighed. 'Okay, if we died right now, which isn't going to happen by the way, Nathan, because my plan is brilliant, then I wouldn't have spent a single night with the woman I love.'

'With who?' Nathan asked, teeth chattering, confused but still trying to keep up.

'With Erin.'

'But you did spent a night with her,' he objected, concentrating fiercely. 'Last night. We all slept together after the fire.'

'So we did,' he agreed. 'I'd forgotten that. Okay, then, but I'm thinking I want more than that. I want lots of nights. And then when I saw those footprints leading to the rocks and I thought I might have lost you…both…' His voice cracked and it was all Erin could do to stay sitting still—which was sensible—and not launch herself into his arms—which wasn't.

'So I'm admitting it,' he said. 'I'm in love. Love at first sight. It's crazy. I don't believe it for a minute but it seems to have happened. Nathan, tell Erin I'm a very sensible person. Tell her I never take risks.'

'So climbing round here rather than wait for the helicopter…'

'Except when they're absolutely necessary for survival of the people I love. You know, my love, that my mother fell in love at first sight, over and over again. It made me think it could never be true. But when I saw your footprints disappearing onto rock, I figured she had it right all along. Her choices were lousy but the concept still holds. I've fallen in love with you, I'll do anything it takes to keep you with me for ever, and I'm saying it here and now…you're necessary for my survival.'

'You don't… You can't know what you're talking about.'

'I don't,' he said, and smiled again, that heart-stopping smile she loved so much. She could see it clear as day in the moonlight, or maybe she could feel it, but she knew it was directed straight at her. Crooked and teasing and just a little bit wicked. 'Teach me,' he said. 'Teach me about loving.'

Wow!

They could have fun, she thought suddenly, a little bit breathlessly. She and this man…

They could have a family. Or maybe they already had a family.

They could have a bigger family.

'I love you, too,' she said, so fast her tongue tripped over itself. She grinned back at him, a great dopy grin. A little bit misty. 'Boy, do my parents have some readjusting to do.'

'I can't wait to meet them.'

A wave, bigger than the rest, smashed into their rock. Their hold on each other tightened. Whatever happened, they were in this together.

Out to sea a fishing boat had rounded the headland. Its flood-lights were playing over the cliffs. The light hit what the fisher-men were looking for—and steadied.

A man, a woman and a child. The child somehow squashed between the adults.

The man kissing the woman as if he'd never let go.

A man, a woman and a child—a family.

The helicopter arrived fifteen minutes after the floodlight hit them. The waves were starting to constitute a serious threat but rescue was on time. Skilled search and rescue personnel were lowered with harnesses, lifting first Nathan, then Erin and finally Dom.

Graham had what seemed to be the entire community on top of the cliff, waiting for them. Every searcher in the district must have got the news and hotfooted it to the scene to be in on this happy ending. Dom saw them all as he was lowered into their midst.

Did these people ever sleep?

Ruby was there, too, holding a sleepy Martin. Reaching to hug him, with Martin squished in the middle.

'Ugh,' Martin said. 'You're wet.'

'And cold,' said a paramedic he recognised, coming toward him with a thermal blanket.

'I'm fine,' Dom said, waving away help. He was searching the crowd for who he needed to find. 'Erin and Nathan?'

'We're warming them inside the ambulance,' the paramedic told him. 'Nathan's bordering on hypothermia. We're guessing, though, that you won't want us to take him to hospital.'

'What's the use of having two doctors if we can't take care of our own.' But Dom was pretty cold himself, and the paramedic was focusing on him as a patient now—not as a doctor.

'Yeah, well, we'll strip you off and get you warm or we're going nowhere,' the guy told him, and Ruby was concurring.

'You do as we say or I'll take you to Campbelltown Hospital myself,' she said.

'You and whose army?'

'Any cheek and I'll box your ears,' she said, and he thought she just might.

'Um…you're not supposed to be here,' Dom said, trying to get his head round what was happening.

'I knew you'd be rescued and Martin and I wanted to see,' Ruby told him. 'And we both want to see you with Erin.'

'You want to see…'

'Our happy ending,' she said serenely. 'Go on, then. There's blankets and warmth and no wind in the ambulance. Oh, and did I mention Erin's in there?' She grinned at the paramedics. 'Take him away, boys. But leave the doors open.'

He had no choice. He was propelled into the back of the ambulance.

Erin was sitting on one of the stretchers. She was draped in thick, warm blankets. Nathan was snuggled close by her side.

'Kiss the girl, Doc,' someone called from the back of the crowd.

'Right,' Dom said drily, and tried to close the doors. But the paramedic was holding the doors firmly open.

'I reckon you have to give the people their money's worth,' he said, chuckling. 'The guys on the boat said you were kissing when they found you. The news has gone round the town and back again. Most of these people have been trekking through bushland to find the kiddie. They want a happy ending.'

'Like you kissing the girl,' someone called out. 'Like in all the best movies.'

'Kiss the new doc,' someone else called.

Hell.

He didn't do emotion—until tonight. He didn't do connection—until tonight, and he surely hadn't ever done public displays of the same. Dominic Spencer was a man who walked alone.

Right. When Erin was huddled under her blanket looking out at him, smiling and smiling. When Nathan was waving to Martin. When Ruby was looking on with her 'get on with it, boy' expression and when this whole amazing community was watching. Waiting for him to kiss their *new* doc.

What was the use of arguing?

And why would he want to?

Walking alone was for idiots, he decided, right there, right then. He tossed it aside along with any last reservations about love at first sight.

So, taking that all into account, there didn't appear to be a choice. He couldn't stand up in the ambulance anyway.

So he knelt. On one knee.

'Erin Carmody, will you take my hand in marriage?' he asked, and there was a collective gasp from the assembled crowd.

Erin's eyes were dancing. 'You idiot.'

'Is that any way to greet a proposal?'

'I don't know. This is only my second. I need a few more to practise with.'

'You can't have any more. I love you.'

She smiled mistily down at him. 'I love your kids,' she ventured.

He met her and raised. 'I love your dog.'

'And I love your town. Oh, and Ruby's fabulous.'

'Erin?' he said, deciding it was time to get things back on track.

'Mmm?'

'I've asked you to marry me.'

'You don't believe in love at first sight.'

'I've known you for three days. That's the longest courtship I'll tolerate. So...' He was starting to sound exasperated. 'Will you marry me?

'Only if you'll share.'

'Share what?'

'Your kids, your house, your patients.' Her laughter faded. 'Your dreams, your fears. Yourself. You.'

'I will,' he said, and there was that something in his voice that told the crowd of onlookers that this was a vow he meant for life.

Erin's misty smile grew even more misty. Her heart was singing, a silly joyous song, a great wonderful chorus. A song of love.

'Will you?' he said.

And then there was nothing for a girl to do. Her crazy, wonderful doctor. Her saviour. Her love.

He was waiting for an answer.

She glanced out at their entranced onlookers. 'You realise there's no way you'll get out of this one.'

'Why would I want to?'

'Why indeed?' she whispered. She slid down onto the cramped floor of the van so she was kneeling right in front of him. She took his hands in hers and she held, as she'd hold for life.

'I do,' she whispered, and then louder, so the audience up the back could hear. 'I do,' she repeated, and she would have said it for a third time but she was caught up and kissed so thoroughly that her third response was lost to everyone but themselves.

'I do.'

And she did.

It involved almost military-like manoeuvres, but they honeymooned alone.

Ruby took Martin and Nathan to Dolphin Bay, promising them a month of beach and sun and fun. 'They'll have a ball,' Dom told his bride—and he sounded almost wistful.

'You don't want to go, too?'

He'd smiled and shaken his head. 'Not this time. Dolphin Bay's the best place in the world if you're a kid in trouble, but I have a better place to take my wife.'

And he was free to take her.

For, amazingly, Charles had offered to take care of the medical needs of Bombadeen while Tansy dog-sat. Bombadeen had been seeing a lot of Charles lately.

Tansy had even caught her bouquet.

There were developments with the kids, too. Applications

had been made to make Dom and Erin into Martin and Nathan's long-term foster-parents. Nathan's dad was in gaol, and likely to remain there. Martin's mother had been sighted in Nepal, and no other parent was in the picture. So it was settled. When their honeymoon was over, Dom and Erin could return to Bombadeen, gather their family and move forward.

For both Erin and Dom, it felt like life had started the moment Erin had walked into his house. He'd opened the door and she'd walked into his heart. Into the heart of his kids. Into the heart of his community.

Sentimental? Maybe it was.

The wedding had been fantastic. They'd done the full bridal bit. Erin had let her somewhat bewildered mother indulge every last fantasy on her wedding dress and there'd never been such a magnificent frock. She had been all lace and flounces and swirling skirts.

It had been crazy. She'd loved it, and so had Dom.

Dom had looked pretty damned handsome, too. A tuxedo, no less. The sight of them together had made her mother cry, but the tears had been tears of joy.

Her parents loved Dominic. After the first shock…well, why wouldn't they?

What else? Tansy was taking two of Marilyn's pups. One for her and one for Charles. Erin was giving the third to her parents to keep Peppy company.

The thought made her chuckle—as so many things made her chuckle these days.

And now… This was the first night of their honeymoon.

They were about as far from Bombadeen as it was possible to be. 'For I'm not sharing my honeymoon with anyone,' Dom growled and Erin agreed entirely.

He'd found a wonderful tropical hideaway—a room built on stilts over a lagoon so beautiful she hardly believed it was real. They'd flown here in normal travelling clothes but Dom had insisted they bring their wedding finery. Tonight, just for themselves, they dressed again.

'For now is the time for us,' Dom decreed, and it was.

So as the sun set over the water, they dressed in full bridal wear.

Erin needed help with the finishing touches. Dom helped her fasten the garland of tiny pink ribbon roses into her hair, then kissed the nape of her neck so gently she sighed with pure, erotic pleasure. There, it was done. Once again they were bride and groom.

A discreet waiter brought them dinner and ice-cold champagne. They dined out on their tiny balcony overlooking the lagoon.

The waiter disappeared. There was nothing but the water lapping gently underneath them, fireflies flitting over the water, moonlight and starlight reflected on the sea, and nothing else.

Except each other.

'We fell in love at first sight,' Dom said softly, raising his champagne flute in her honour. 'We have all our lives to get to know each other.'

'I believe I know you already,' Erin said softly. 'I knew you the moment I saw you. My heart knew you.'

'That's corny,' he said, and smiled.

'So it is.'

'True, though.' He pushed back his chair. 'Would you like to dance, my love?'

'I believe I would,' she whispered, and they did, a long slow waltz with no music but the music that was inside them.

He held her close. Against his heart.

'So where's the man who walks alone now?' she teased, holding him against her, savouring the feel of his body holding her close. Her dress was swishing around them in delicious folds of silk and lace. She was a white cloud on a starlit night. There was nothing and no one but man and wife. In love.

'Maybe I never was alone,' he whispered into her hair. 'Maybe from the time Ruby took me in, from the time her care made me want to take in kids, from the time you walked into my life, from the time I decided to be a dog breeder... Where does love start?'

'Where does it end?'

'It never ends,' he whispered, swinging her round and round and round. 'And you know the lovely thing about family?'

'What?'

'We can use 'em,' he said in quiet satisfaction. 'We may have kids and dogs but we also have your parents and Ruby and Tansy and Charles. That's five great kid sitters. So whenever I want my wife entirely to myself...'

'Why would you want that?'

He chuckled. 'Why indeed? Let me show you.' He lifted her high into his arms and held her against his heart. They gazed together out over the starlit water, and then, firmly, Dom turned his back on the loveliness of the night. He carried his wife into their luxurious room, where a great wide bed was waiting. There were crisp white sheets, mounds of down-stuffed pillows, and soft, soft duvets.

What more could two lovers want?

Only each other. He lowered her onto the sheets and started unfastening the tiny buttons at her breast, one by one.

'Such a waste,' she teased softly. 'To take it all off again.'

'And again and again,' he whispered, slipping the dress from her shoulders and sinking to lie beside her. 'For I'll love you again and again, for as long as we both shall live.'

'That sounds just fine to me,' she whispered. She wound her arms around his neck and tugged him forward, so she could kiss him deeply, properly, wonderfully, as a woman should. As a wife should.

'That sounds fabulous,' she whispered. 'As long as I can love you right back.'

MILLS & BOON®
Pure reading pleasure™

JUNE 2009 HARDBACK TITLES

ROMANCE

The Sicilian's Baby Bargain	Penny Jordan
Mistress: Pregnant by the Spanish Billionaire	Kim Lawrence
Bound by the Marcolini Diamonds	Melanie Milburne
Blackmailed into the Greek Tycoon's Bed	Carol Marinelli
The Ruthless Greek's Virgin Princess	Trish Morey
Veretti's Dark Vengeance	Lucy Gordon
Spanish Magnate, Red-Hot Revenge	Lynn Raye Harris
Argentinian Playboy, Unexpected Love-Child	Chantelle Shaw
The Savakis Mistress	Annie West
Captive in the Millionaire's Castle	Lee Wilkinson
Cattle Baron: Nanny Needed	Margaret Way
Greek Boss, Dream Proposal	Barbara McMahon
Boardroom Baby Surprise	Jackie Braun
Bachelor Dad on Her Doorstep	Michelle Douglas
Hired: Cinderella Chef	Myrna Mackenzie
Miss Maple and the Playboy	Cara Colter
A Special Kind of Family	Marion Lennox
Hot Shot Surgeon, Cinderella Bride	Alison Roberts

HISTORICAL

The Rake's Wicked Proposal	Carole Mortimer
The Transformation of Miss Ashworth	Anne Ashley
Mistress Below Deck	Helen Dickson

MEDICAL™

Emergency: Wife Lost and Found	Carol Marinelli
A Summer Wedding at Willowmere	Abigail Gordon
The Playboy Doctor Claims His Bride	Janice Lynn
Miracle: Twin Babies	Fiona Lowe

0509 Gen Std LP

MILLS & BOON®
Pure reading pleasure™

JUNE 2009 LARGE PRINT TITLES

ROMANCE

The Ruthless Magnate's Virgin Mistress	Lynne Graham
The Greek's Forced Bride	Michelle Reid
The Sheikh's Rebellious Mistress	Sandra Marton
The Prince's Waitress Wife	Sarah Morgan
The Australian's Society Bride	Margaret Way
The Royal Marriage Arrangement	Rebecca Winters
Two Little Miracles	Caroline Anderson
Manhattan Boss, Diamond Proposal	Trish Wylie

HISTORICAL

Marrying the Mistress	Juliet Landon
To Deceive a Duke	Amanda McCabe
Knight of Grace	Sophia James

MEDICAL™

A Mummy for Christmas	Caroline Anderson
A Bride and Child Worth Waiting For	Marion Lennox
One Magical Christmas	Carol Marinelli
The GP's Meant-To-Be Bride	Jennifer Taylor
The Italian Surgeon's Christmas Miracle	Alison Roberts
Children's Doctor, Christmas Bride	Lucy Clark

JULY 2009 HARDBACK TITLES

ROMANCE

Marchese's Forgotten Bride	Michelle Reid
The Brazilian Millionaire's Love-Child	Anne Mather
Powerful Greek, Unworldly Wife	Sarah Morgan
The Virgin Secretary's Impossible Boss	Carole Mortimer
Kyriakis's Innocent Mistress	Diana Hamilton
Rich, Ruthless and Secretly Royal	Robyn Donald
Spanish Aristocrat, Forced Bride	India Grey
Kept for Her Baby	Kate Walker
The Costanzo Baby Secret	Catherine Spencer
The Mediterranean's Wife by Contract	Kathryn Ross
Claimed: Secret Royal Son	Marion Lennox
Expecting Miracle Twins	Barbara Hannay
A Trip with the Tycoon	Nicola Marsh
Invitation to the Boss's Ball	Fiona Harper
Keeping Her Baby's Secret	Raye Morgan
Memo: The Billionaire's Proposal	Melissa McClone
Secret Sheikh, Secret Baby	Carol Marinelli
The Playboy Doctor's Surprise Proposal	Anne Fraser

HISTORICAL

The Piratical Miss Ravenhurst	Louise Allen
His Forbidden Liaison	Joanna Maitland
An Innocent Debutante in Hanover Square	Anne Herries

MEDICAL™

Pregnant Midwife: Father Needed	Fiona McArthur
His Baby Bombshell	Jessica Matthews
Found: A Mother for His Son	Dianne Drake
Hired: GP and Wife	Judy Campbell

0609 Gen Std LP

™MILLS & BOON®

Pure reading pleasure™

JULY 2009 LARGE PRINT TITLES

ROMANCE

Captive At The Sicilian Billionaire's Command	Penny Jordan
The Greek's Million-Dollar Baby Bargain	Julia James
Bedded for the Spaniard's Pleasure	Carole Mortimer
At the Argentinean Billionaire's Bidding	India Grey
Italian Groom, Princess Bride	Rebecca Winters
Falling for her Convenient Husband	Jessica Steele
Cinderella's Wedding Wish	Jessica Hart
The Rebel Heir's Bride	Patricia Thayer

HISTORICAL

The Rake's Defiant Mistress	Mary Brendan
The Viscount Claims His Bride	Bronwyn Scott
The Major and the Country Miss	Dorothy Elbury

MEDICAL™

The Greek Doctor's New-Year Baby	Kate Hardy
The Heart Surgeon's Secret Child	Meredith Webber
The Midwife's Little Miracle	Fiona McArthur
The Single Dad's New-Year Bride	Amy Andrews
The Wife He's Been Waiting For	Dianne Drake
Posh Doc Claims His Bride	Anne Fraser